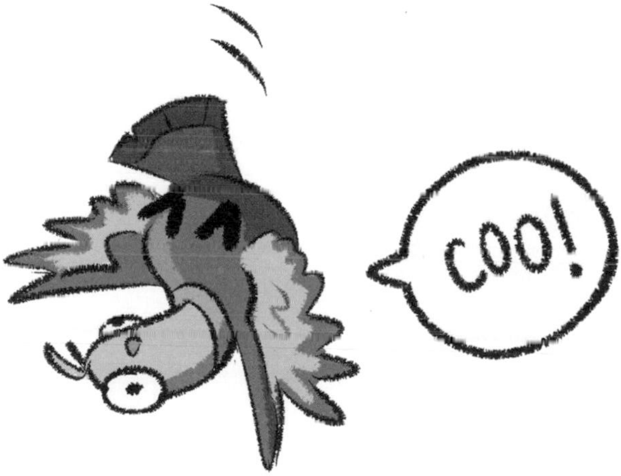
COO!

A MIGHTY MARVEL TEAM-UP

# SPIDER-MAN

## ANIMALS ASSEMBLE!

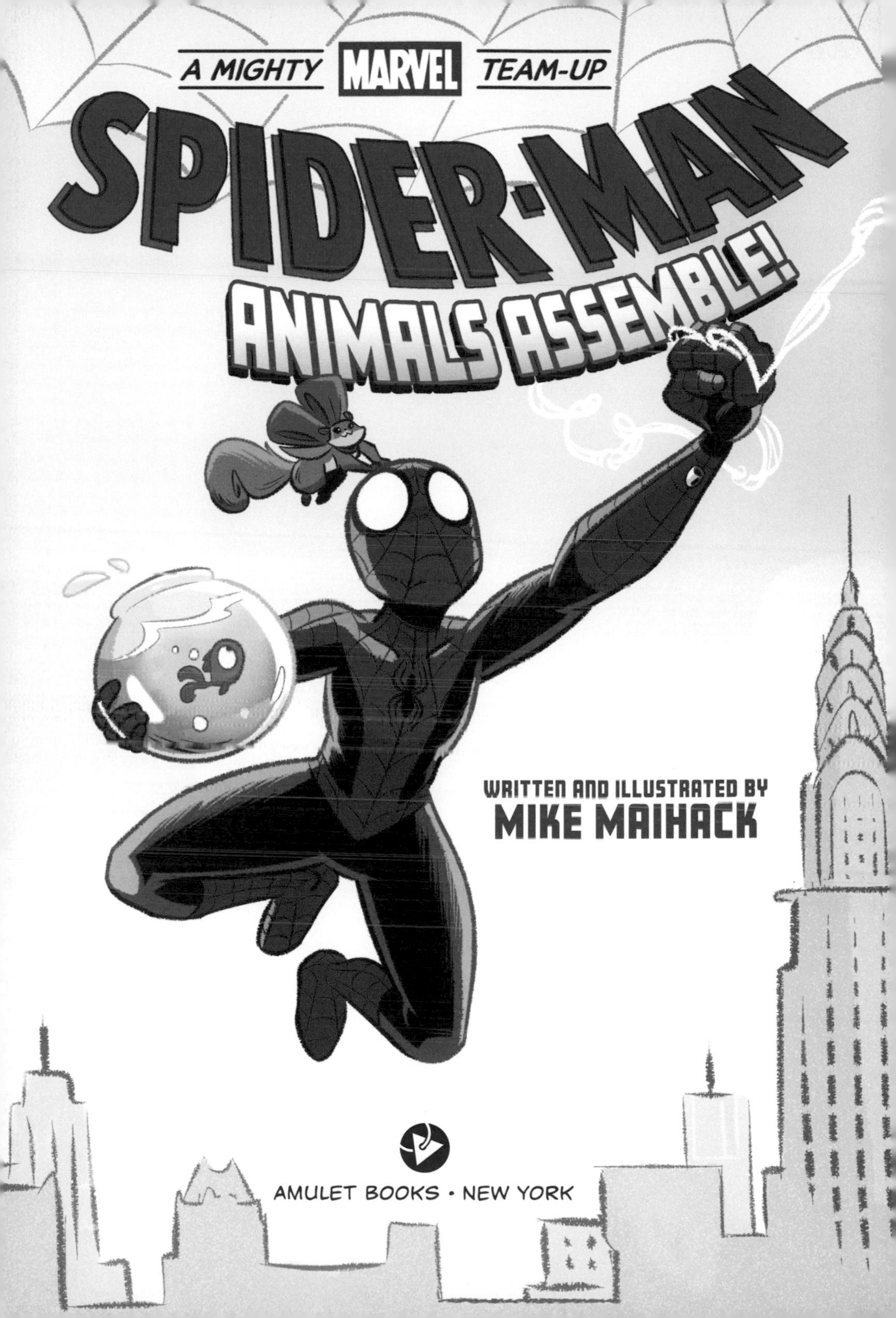


WRITTEN AND ILLUSTRATED BY

MIKE MAIHACK



AMULET BOOKS • NEW YORK

Library of Congress Control Number 2022940920

ISBN 978-1-4197-6480-6

© 2023 MARVEL
Text and illustrations by Mike Maihack
Book design by Brann Garvey

Printed and bound in China
10 9 8 7 6 5 4 3 2 1

Amulet Books are available at special discounts when purchased in quantity for premiums and promotions as well as fundraising or educational use. Special editions can also be created to specification. For details, contact specialsales@abramsbooks.com or the address below.

Amulet Books® is a registered
trademark of Harry N. Abrams, Inc.

**ABRAMS** The Art of Books
195 Broadway, New York, NY 10007
abramsbooks.com

FOR ANYONE WHO'S HAD A
RESPONSIBILITY THEY FELT WAS
TOO BIG OR TOO SMALL TO HANDLE

—M.M.

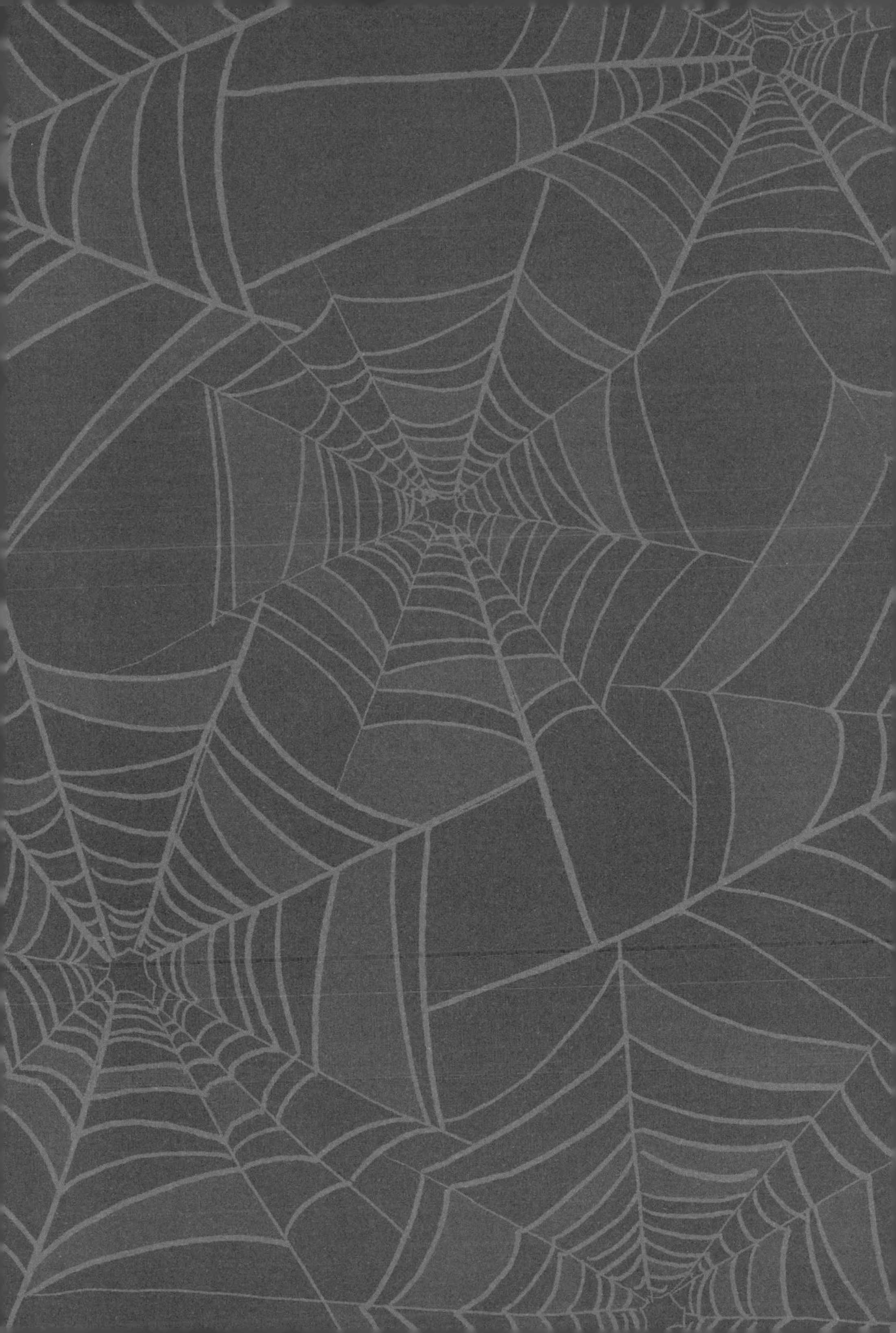

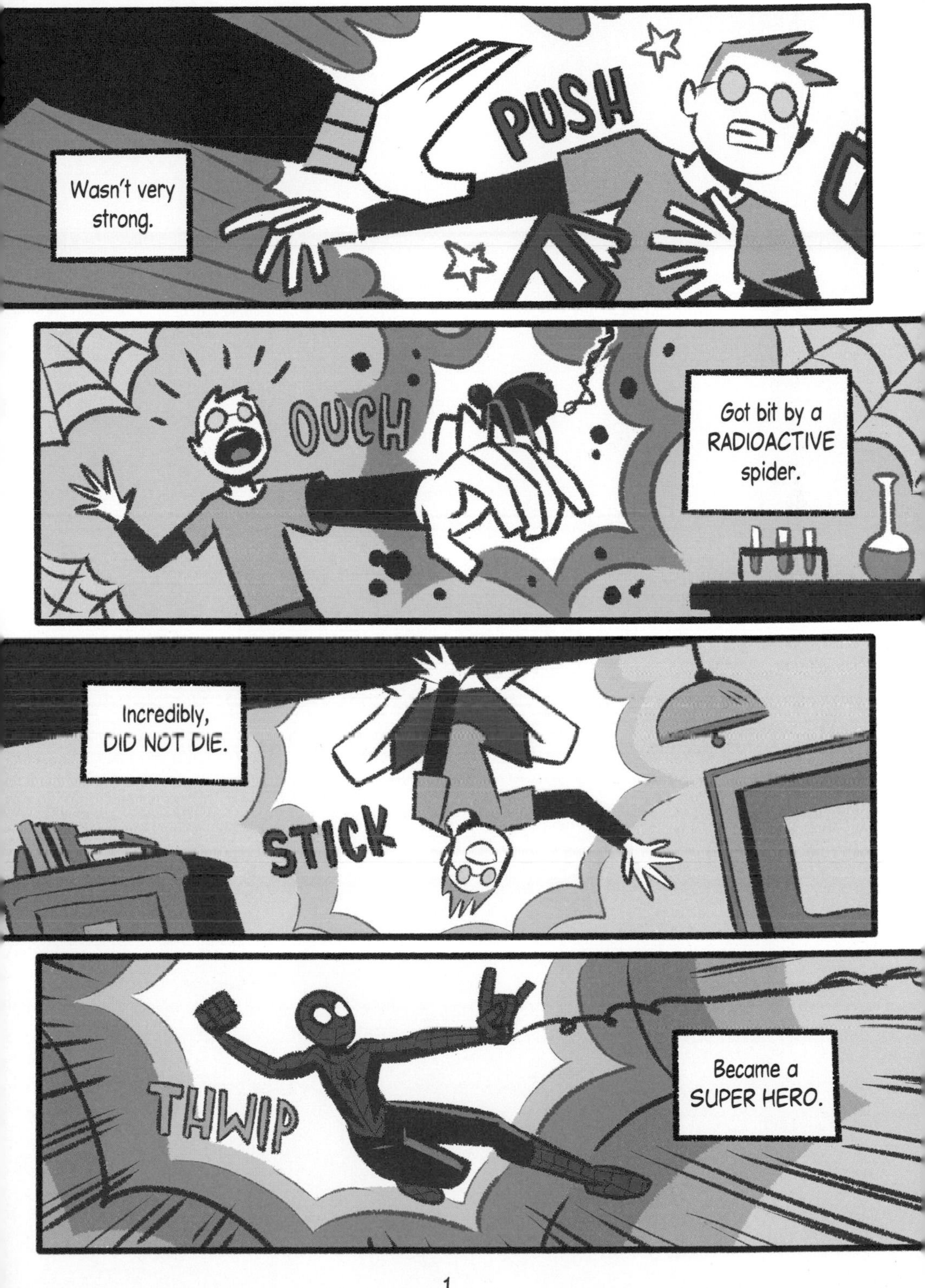
Wasn't very strong.
PUSH
OUCH
Got bit by a RADIOACTIVE spider.
Incredibly, DID NOT DIE.
STICK
THWIP
Became a SUPER HERO.

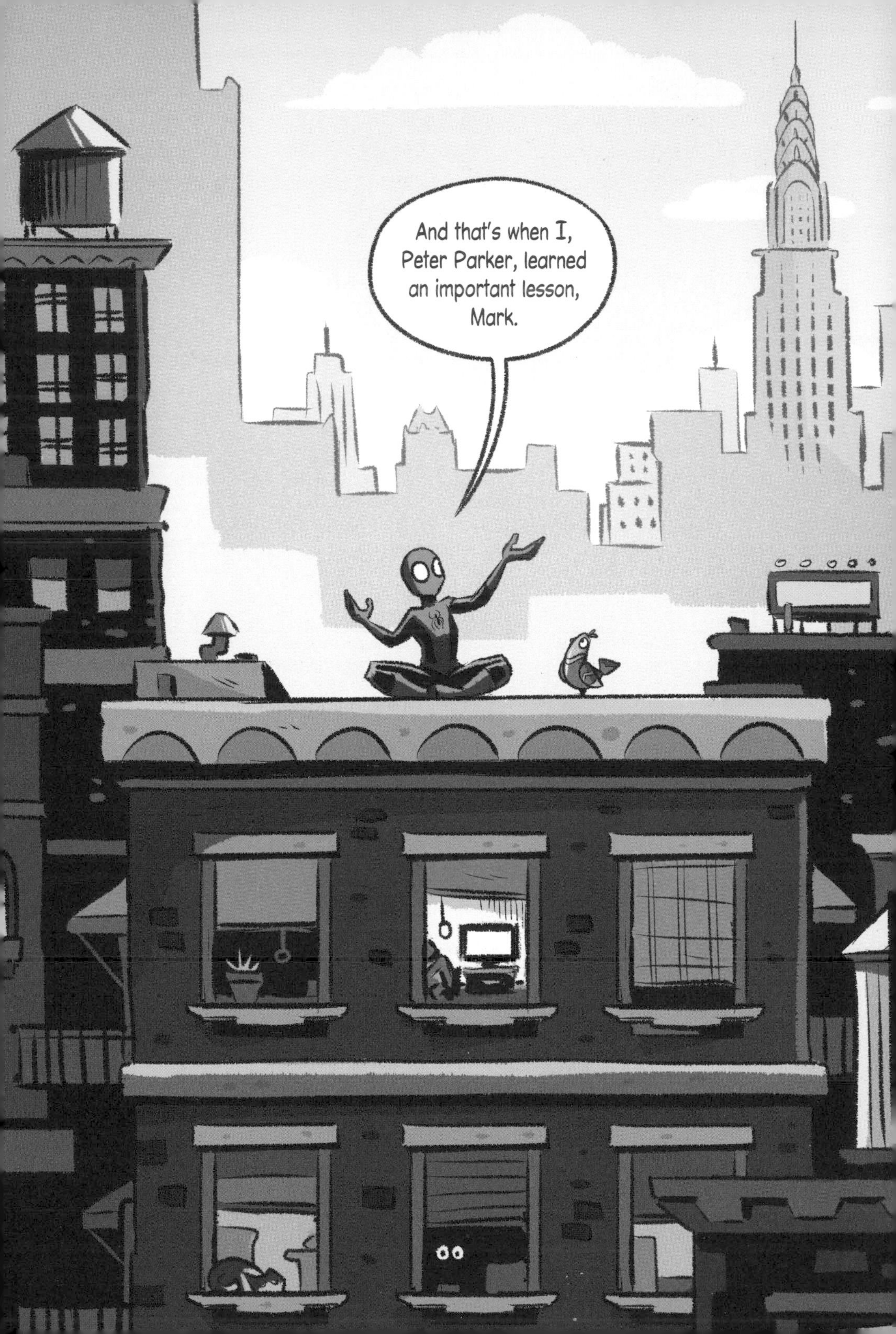
And that's when I, Peter Parker, learned an important lesson, Mark.

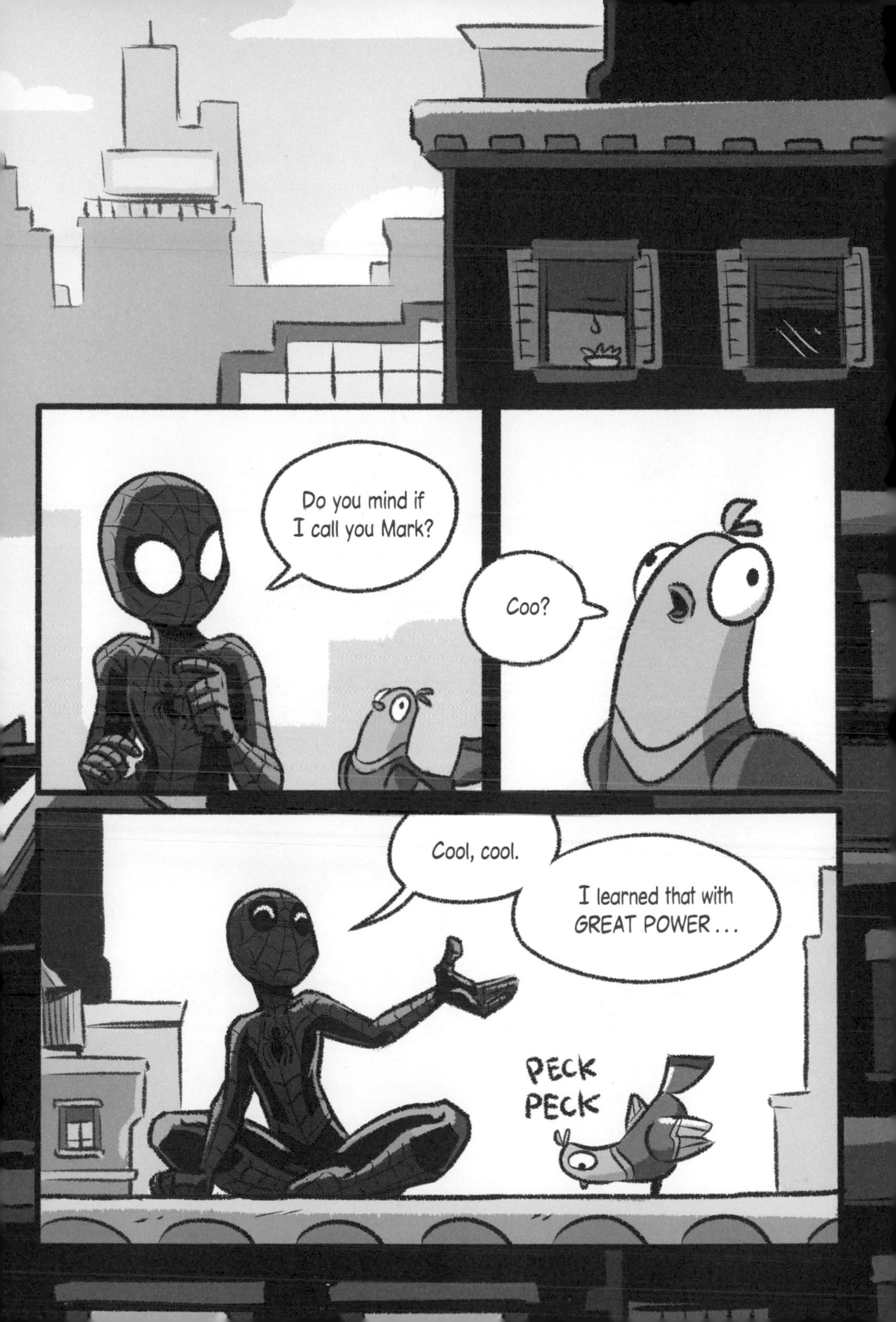
Do you mind if I call you Mark?
Coo?
Cool, cool.
I learned that with GREAT POWER . . .
PECK PECK

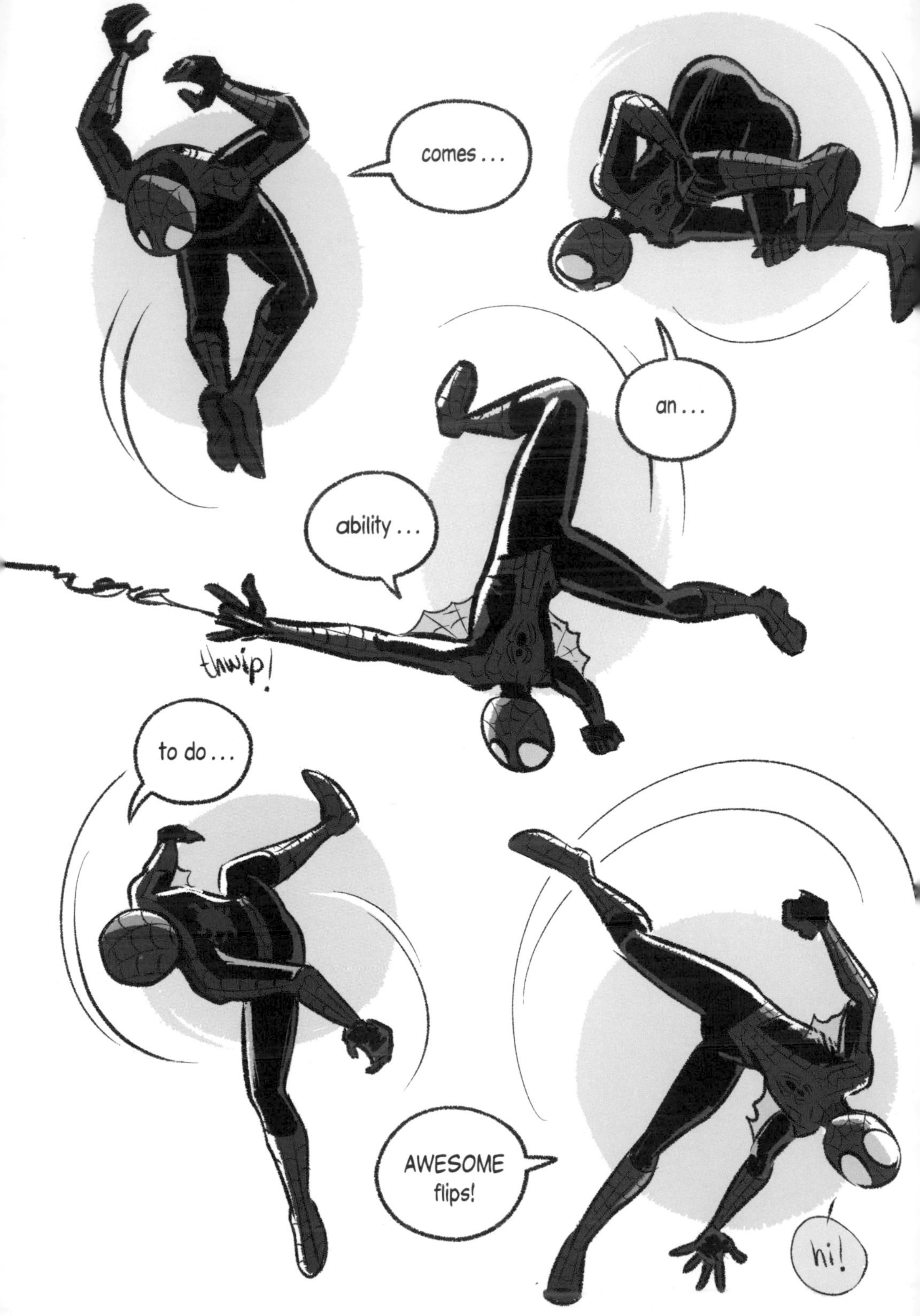
comes . . .
an . . .
ability . . .
thwip!
to do . . .
AWESOME flips!
hi!

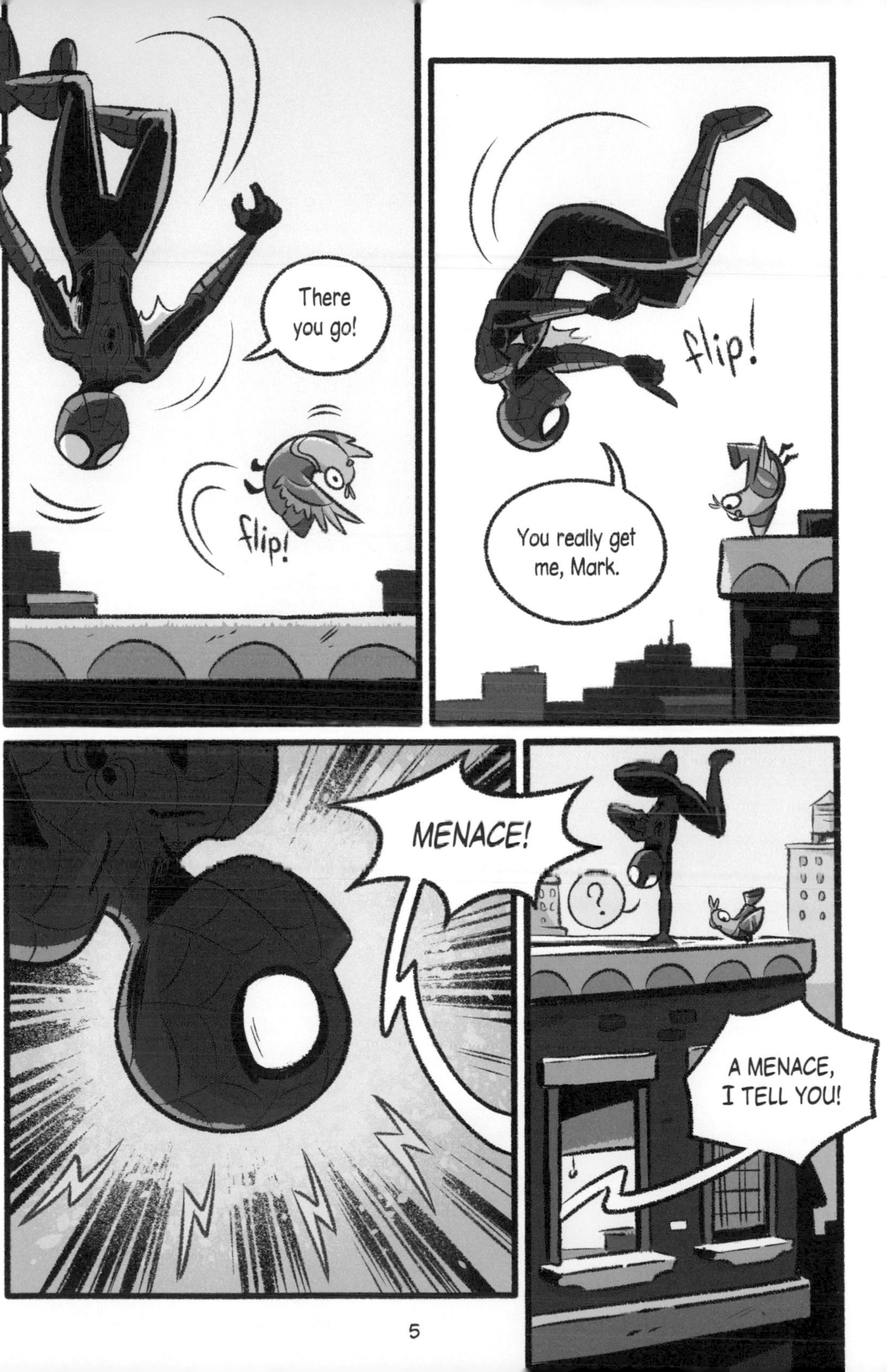

There you go!
flip!
flip!
You really get me, Mark.
MENACE!
?
A MENACE, I TELL YOU!

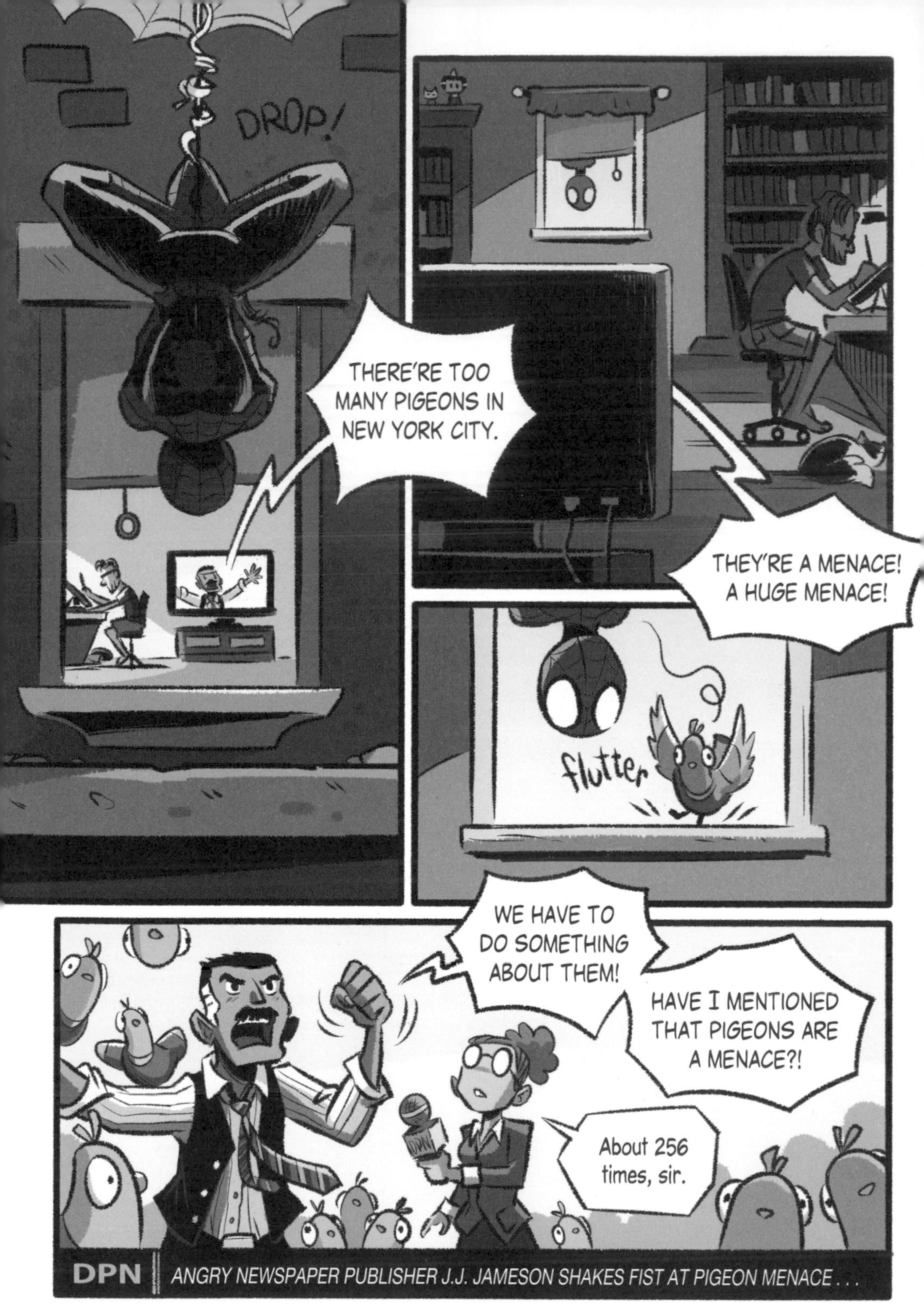
DROP!
THERE'RE TOO MANY PIGEONS IN NEW YORK CITY.
THEY'RE A MENACE! A HUGE MENACE!
flutter
WE HAVE TO DO SOMETHING ABOUT THEM!
HAVE I MENTIONED THAT PIGEONS ARE A MENACE?!
About 256 times, sir.
DPN
ANGRY NEWSPAPER PUBLISHER J.J. JAMESON SHAKES FIST AT PIGEON MENACE . . .

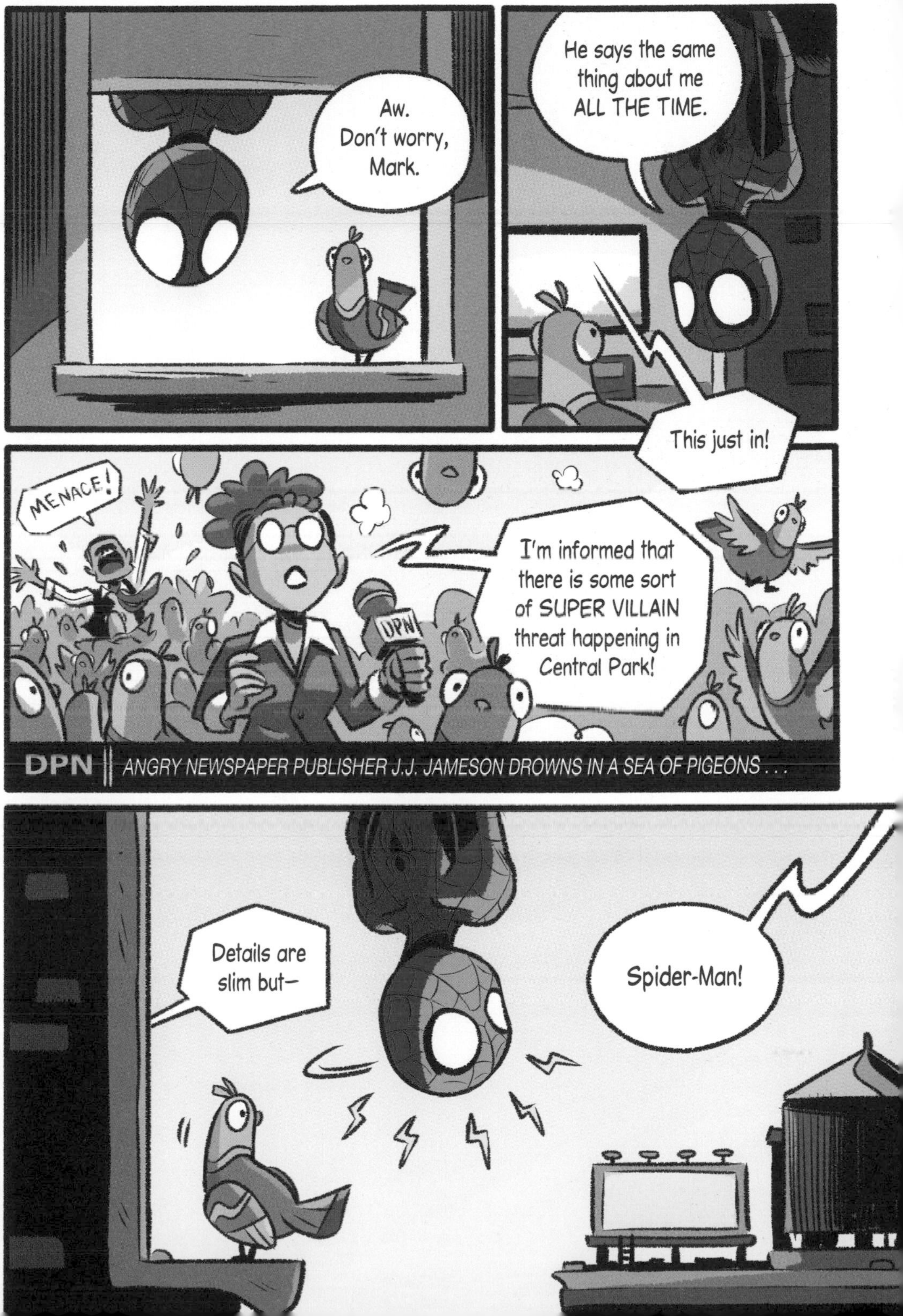
Aw. Don't worry, Mark.
He says the same thing about me ALL THE TIME.
This just in!
MENACE!
DPN
I'm informed that there is some sort of SUPER VILLAIN threat happening in Central Park!
DPN ANGRY NEWSPAPER PUBLISHER J.J. JAMESON DROWNS IN A SEA OF PIGEONS . . .
Details are slim but—
Spider-Man!

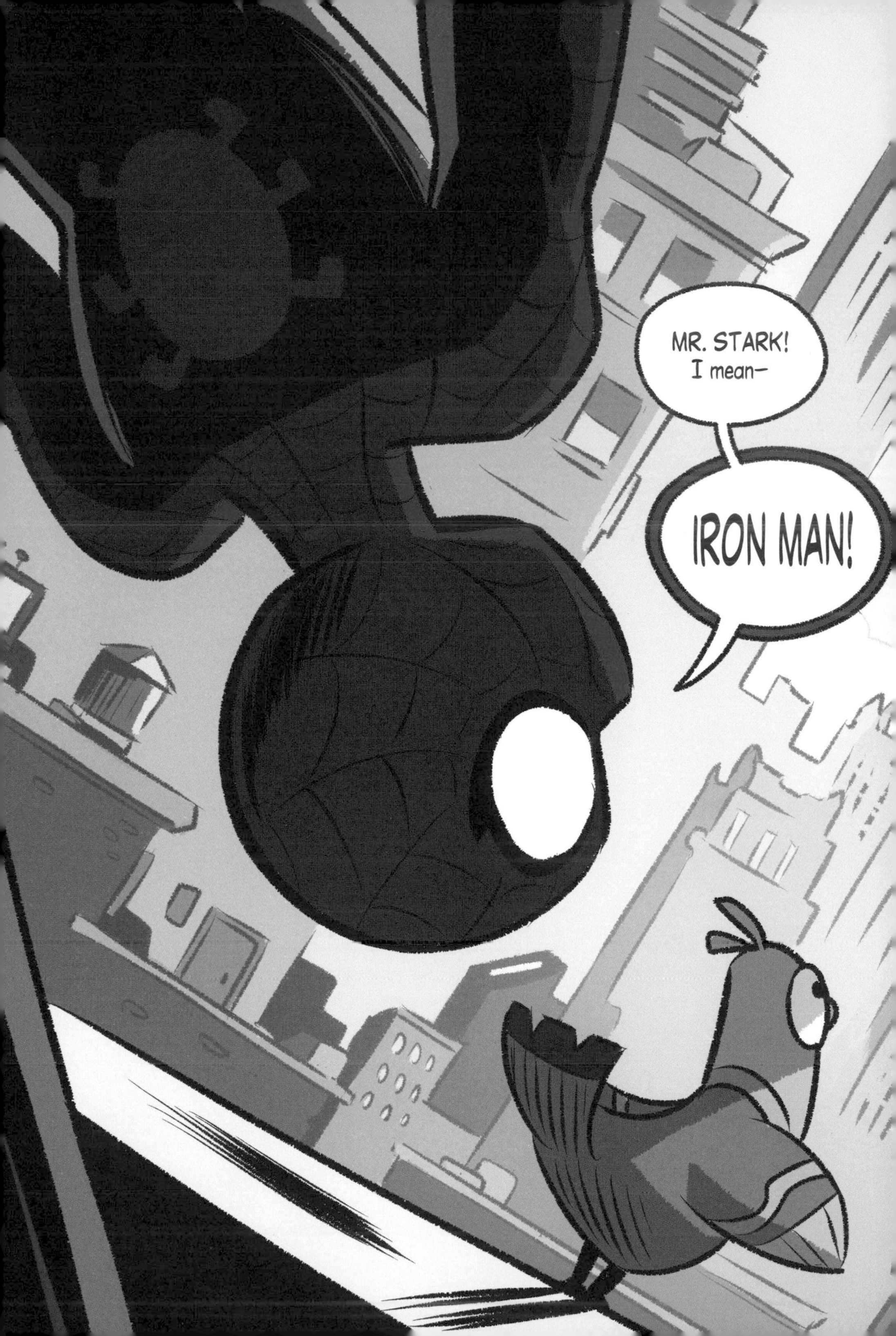
MR. STARK! I mean—
IRON MAN!

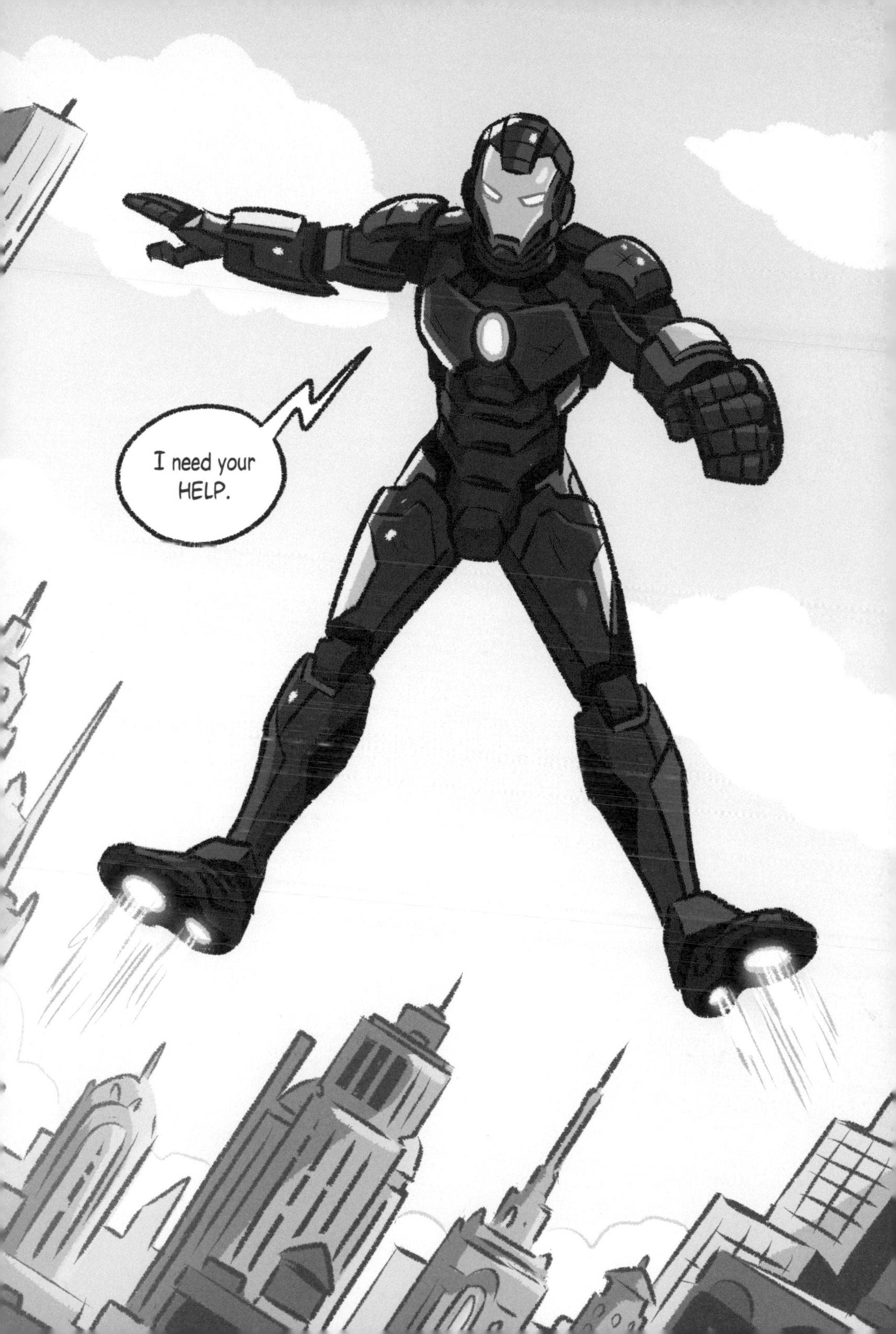
I need your HELP.

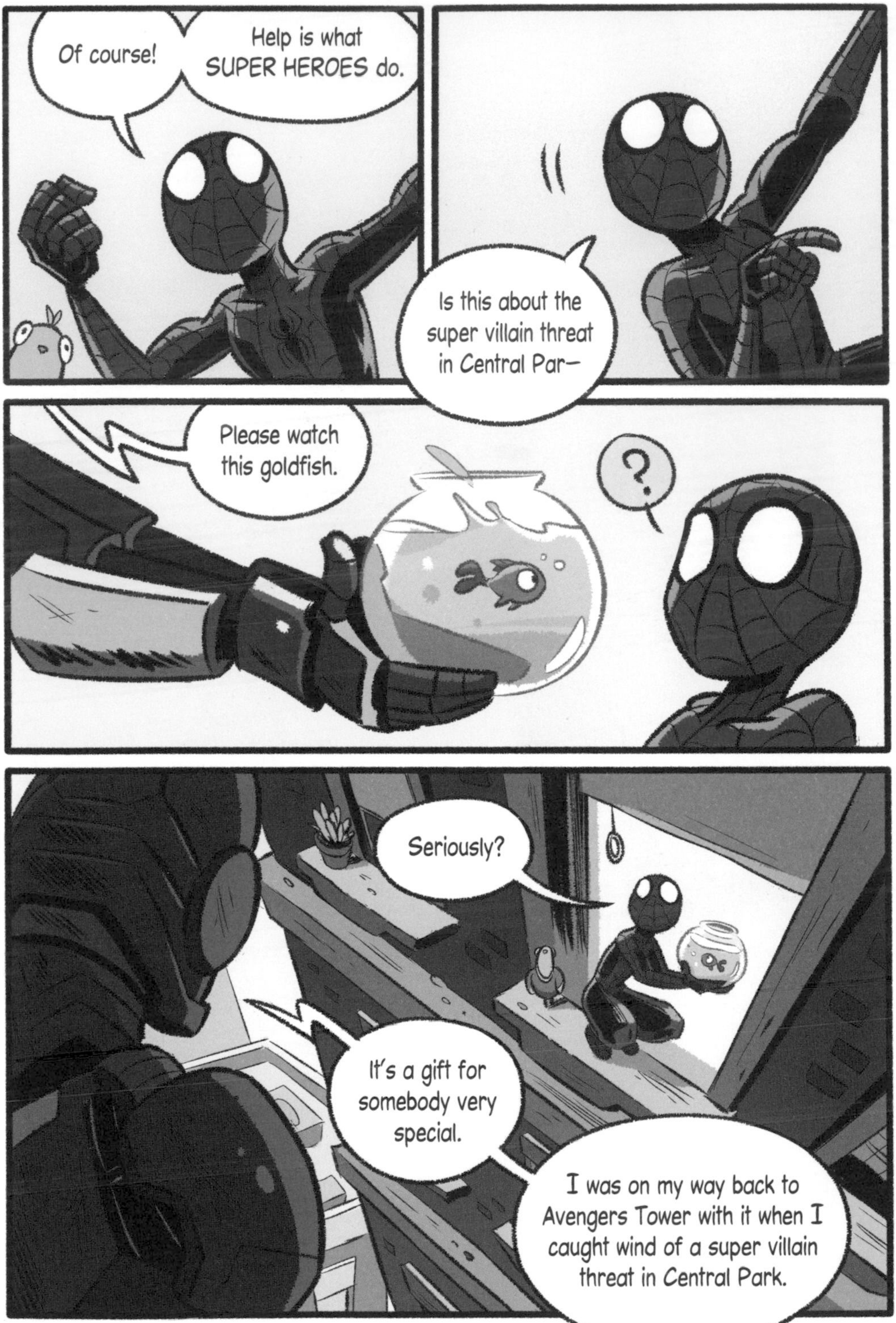
Of course!
Help is what SUPER HEROES do.
Is this about the super villain threat in Central Par—
Please watch this goldfish.
?
Seriously?
It's a gift for somebody very special.
I was on my way back to Avengers Tower with it when I caught wind of a super villain threat in Central Park.

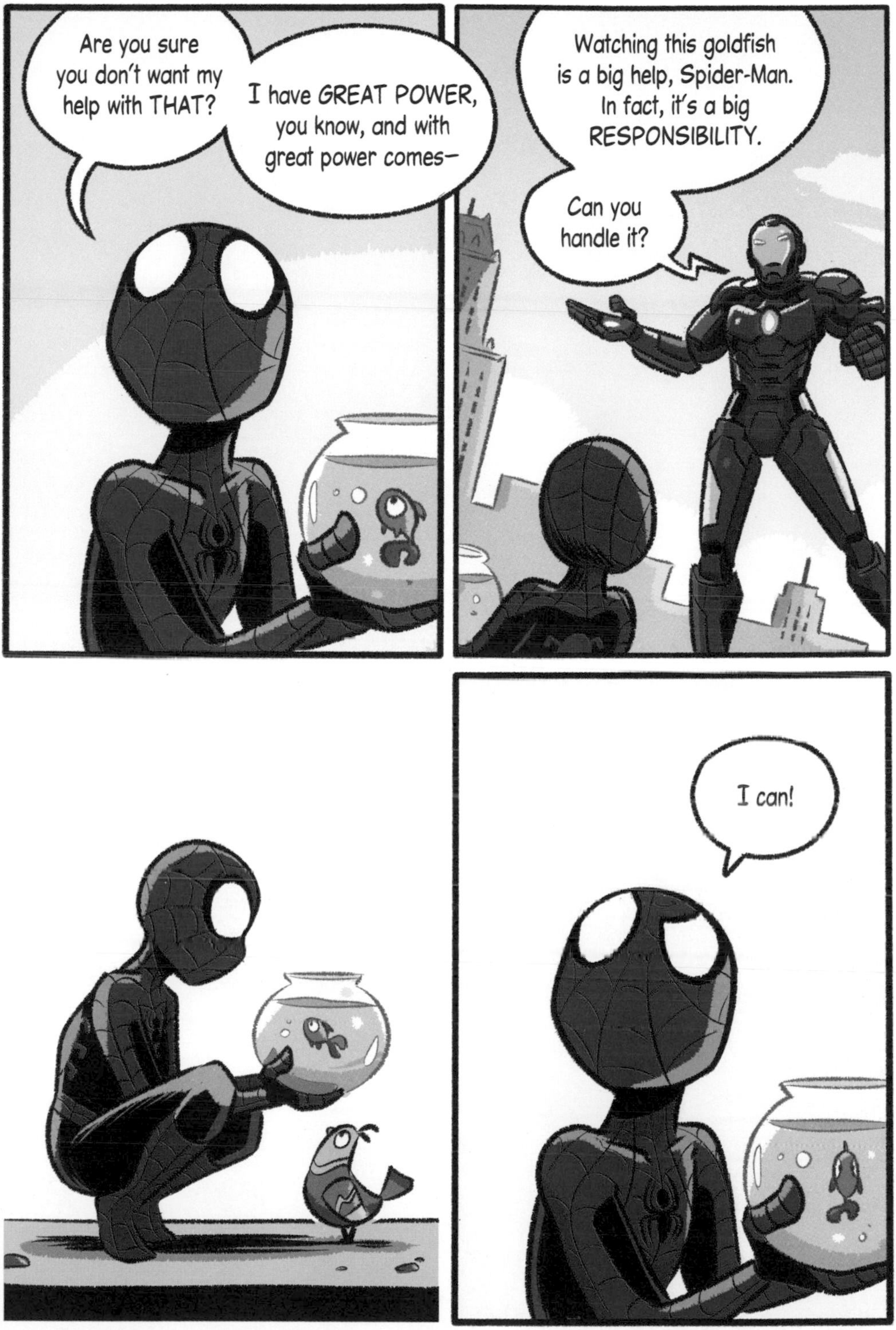
Are you sure you don't want my help with THAT?
I have GREAT POWER, you know, and with great power comes–
Watching this goldfish is a big help, Spider-Man. In fact, it's a big RESPONSIBILITY.
Can you handle it?
I can!

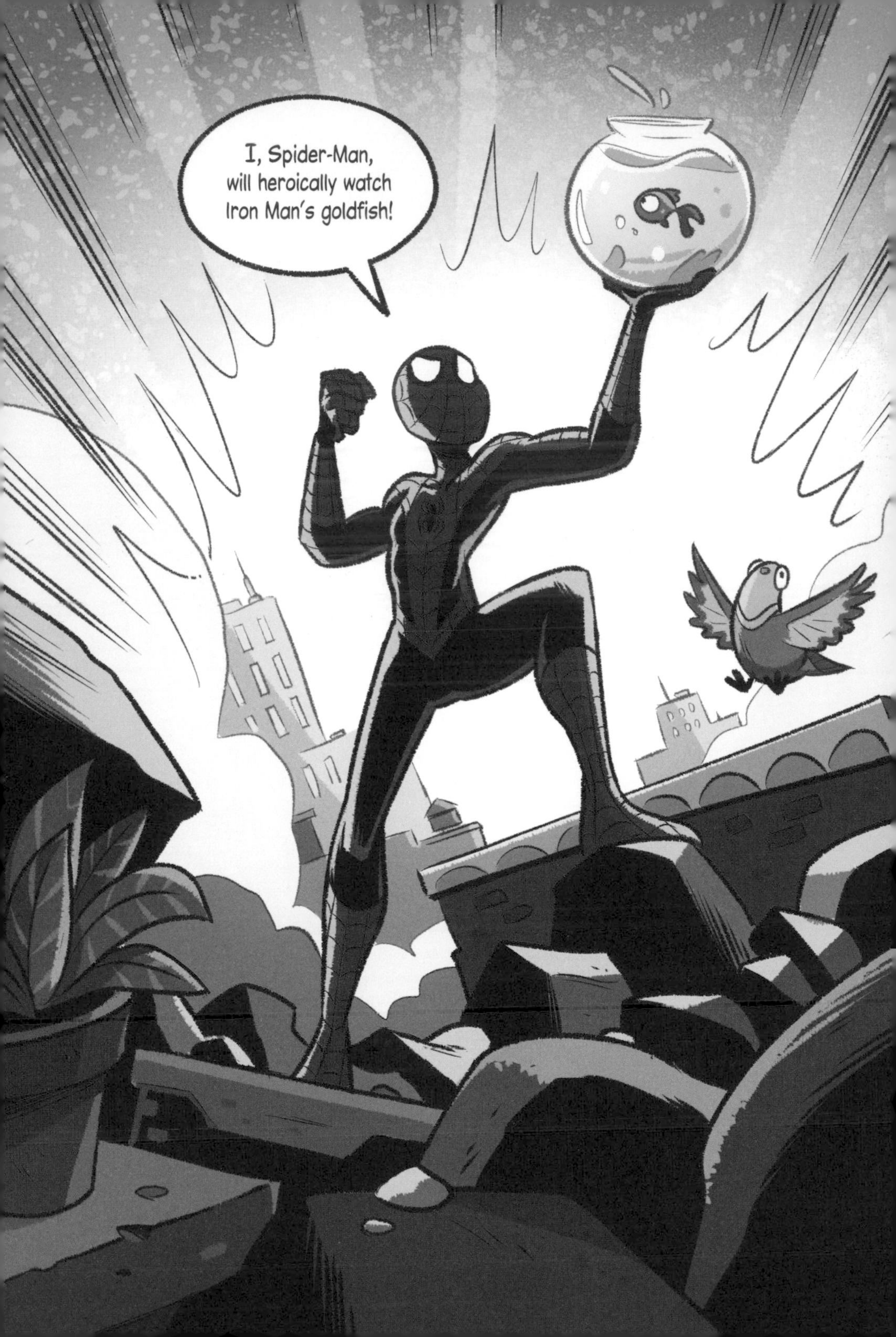
I, Spider-Man, will heroically watch Iron Man's goldfish!

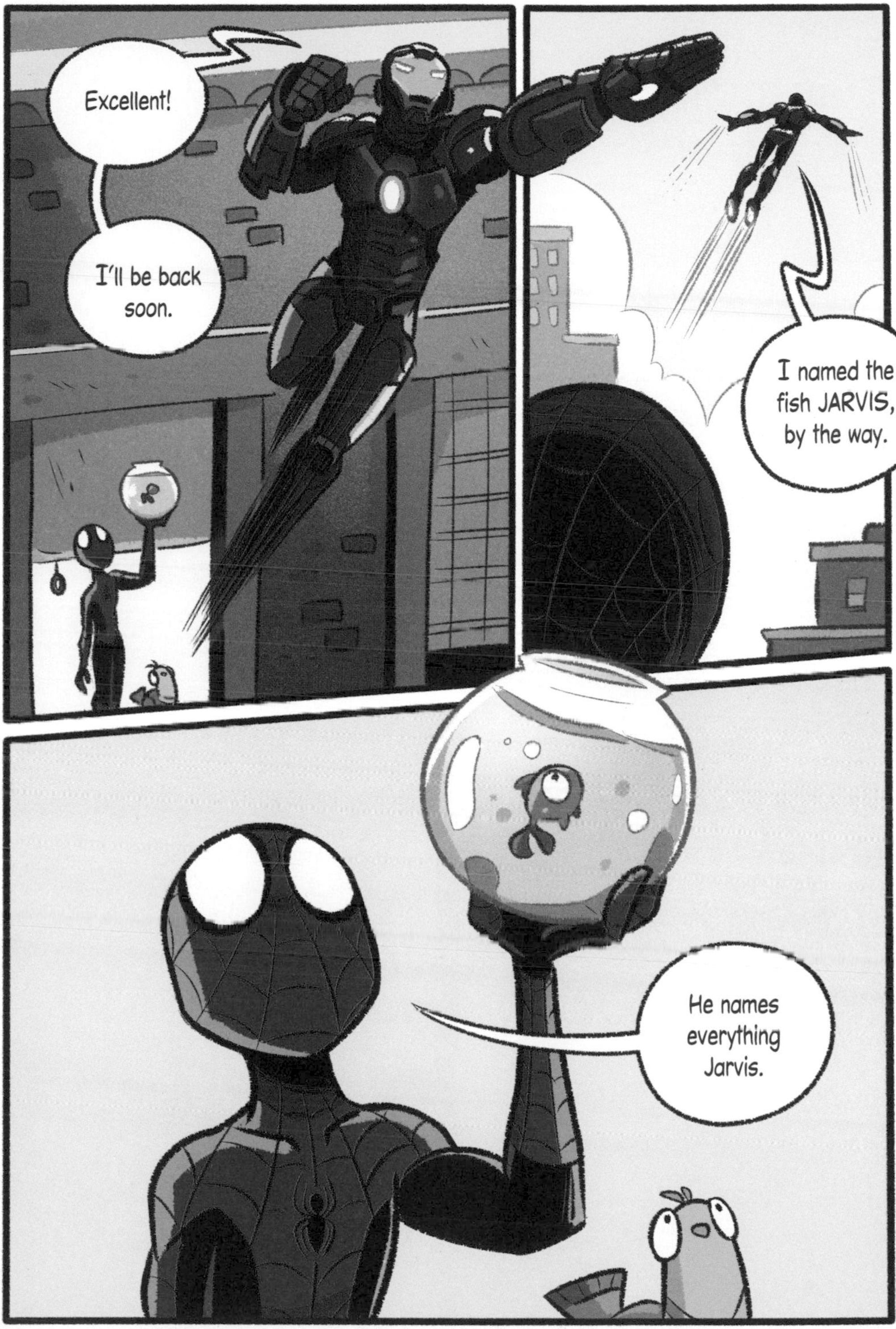
Excellent!
I'll be back soon.
I named the fish JARVIS, by the way.
He names everything Jarvis.

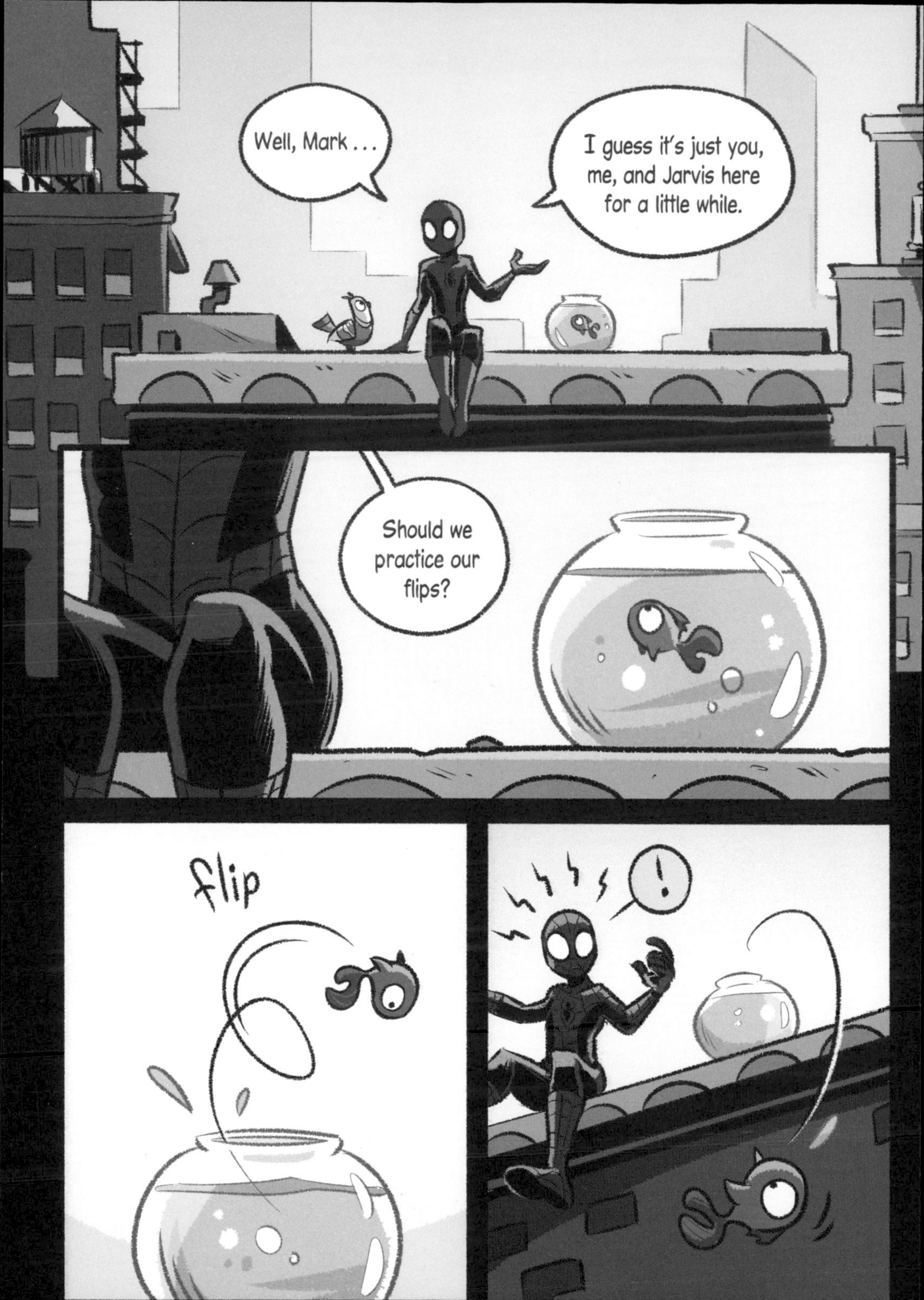
Well, Mark . . .
I guess it's just you, me, and Jarvis here for a little while.
Should we practice our flips?
flip
!

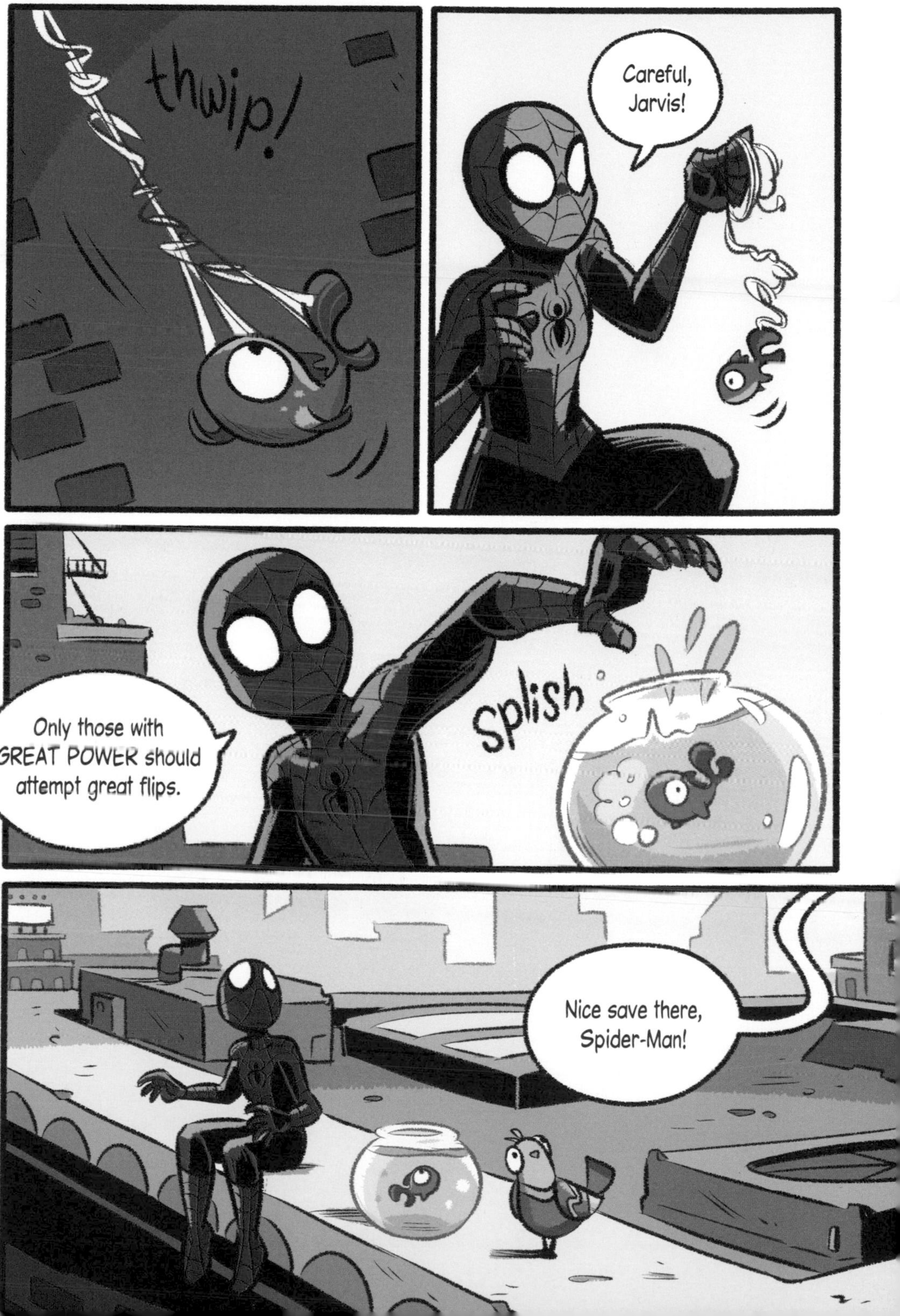
thwip!
Careful, Jarvis!
Only those with GREAT POWER should attempt great flips.
splish
Nice save there, Spider-Man!

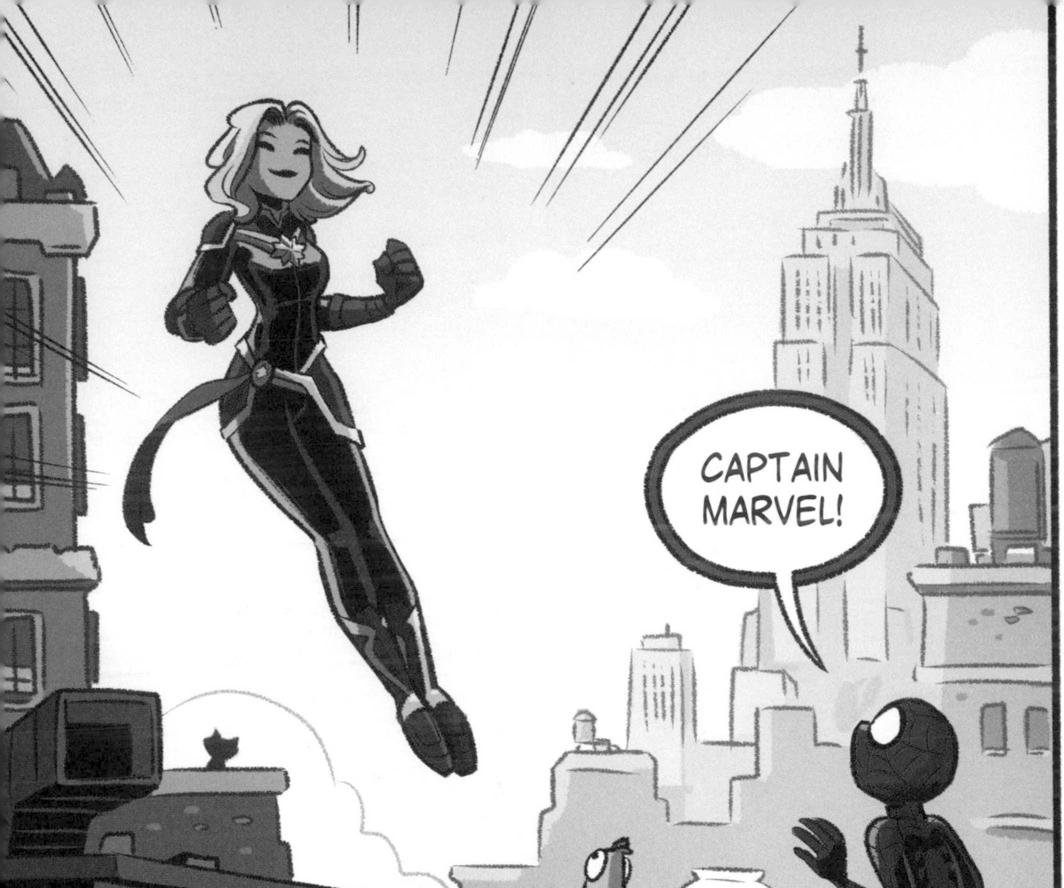
CAPTAIN MARVEL!

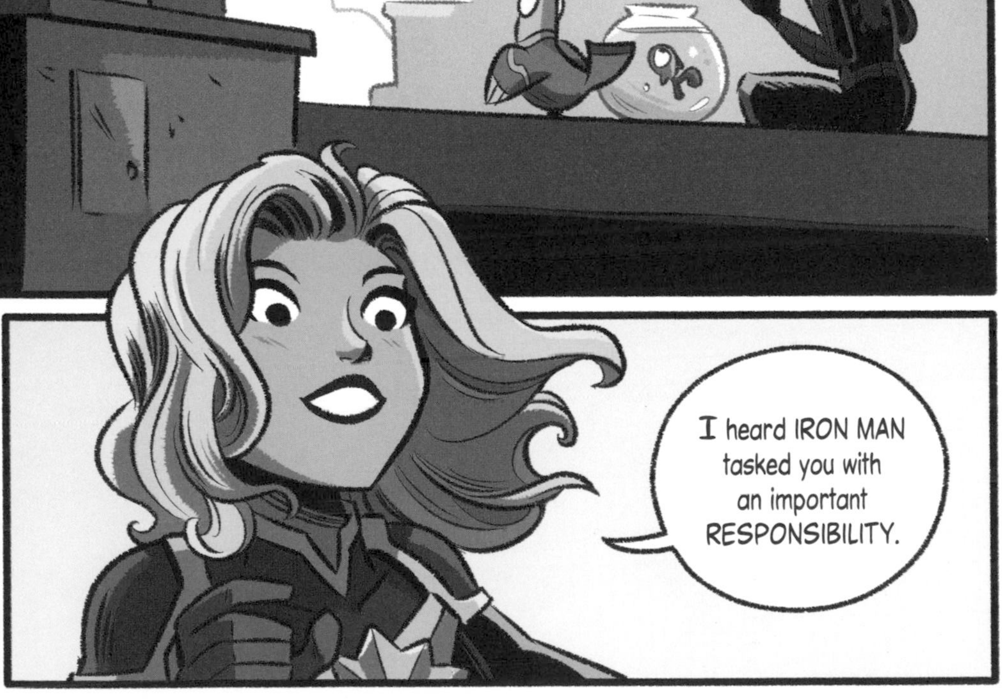
I heard IRON MAN tasked you with an important RESPONSIBILITY.

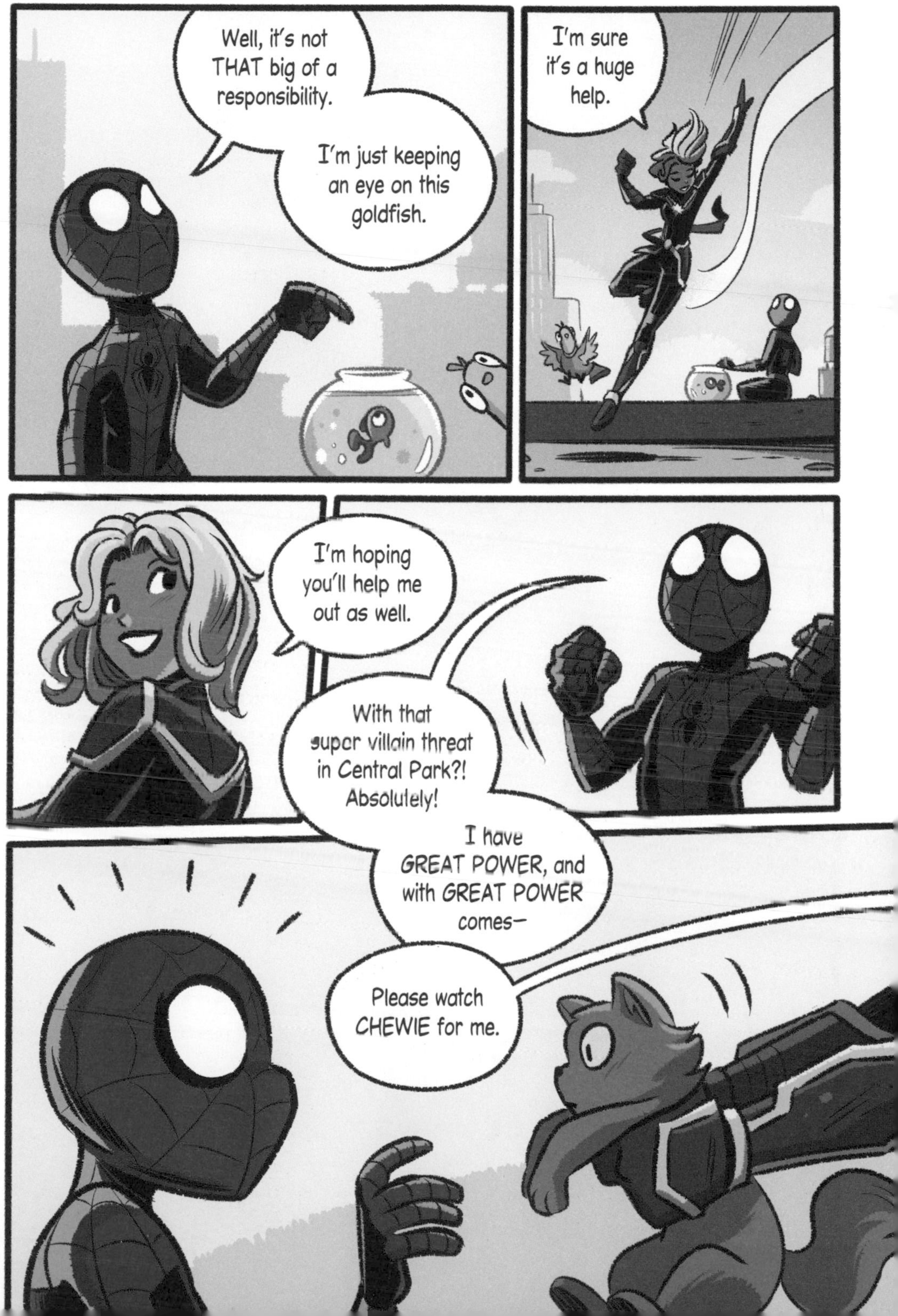

Well, it's not THAT big of a responsibility.
I'm just keeping an eye on this goldfish.
I'm sure it's a huge help.
I'm hoping you'll help me out as well.
With that super villain threat in Central Park?! Absolutely!
I have GREAT POWER, and with GREAT POWER comes—
Please watch CHEWIE for me.

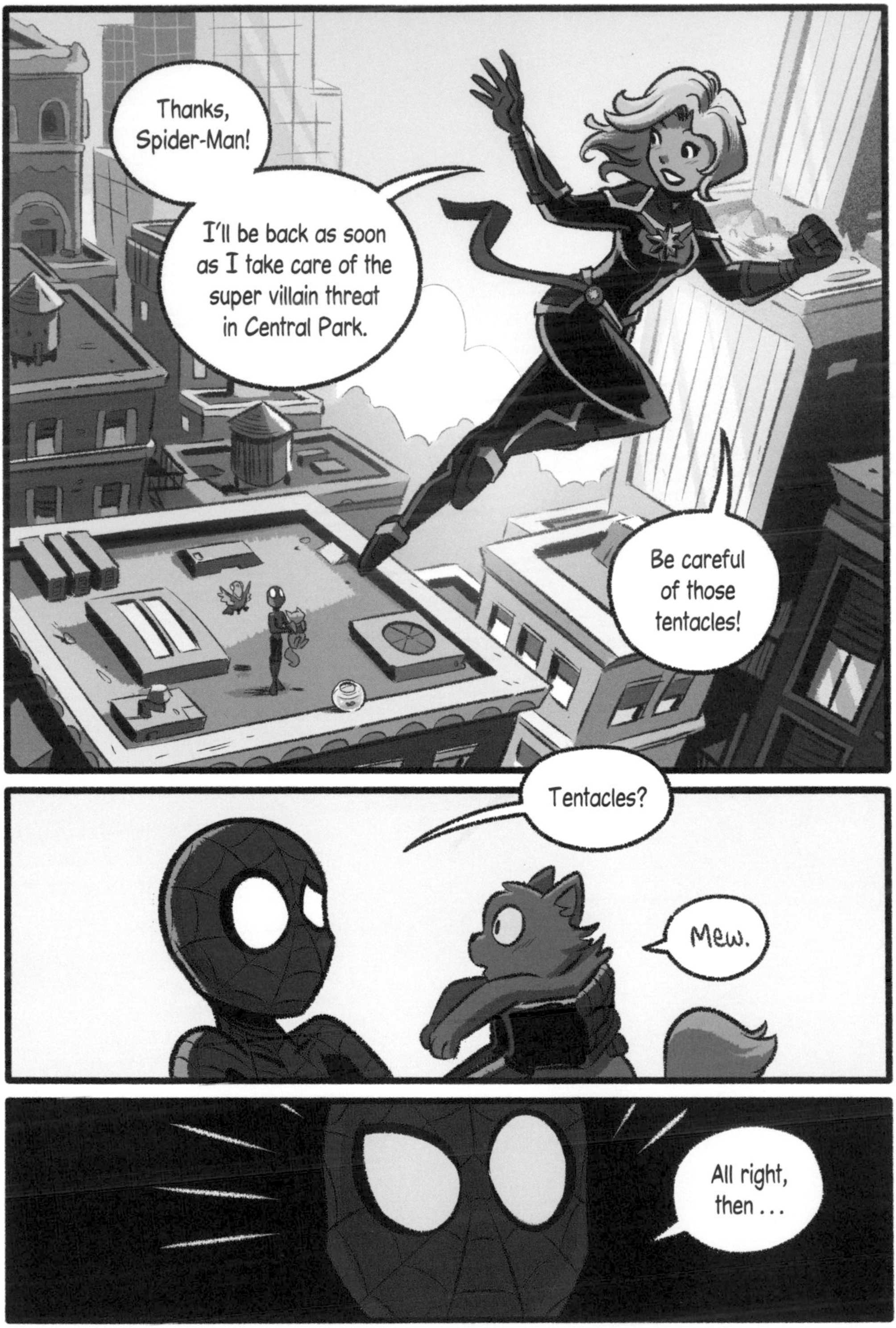
Thanks, Spider-Man!
I'll be back as soon as I take care of the super villain threat in Central Park.
Be careful of those tentacles!
Tentacles?
Mew.
All right, then . . .

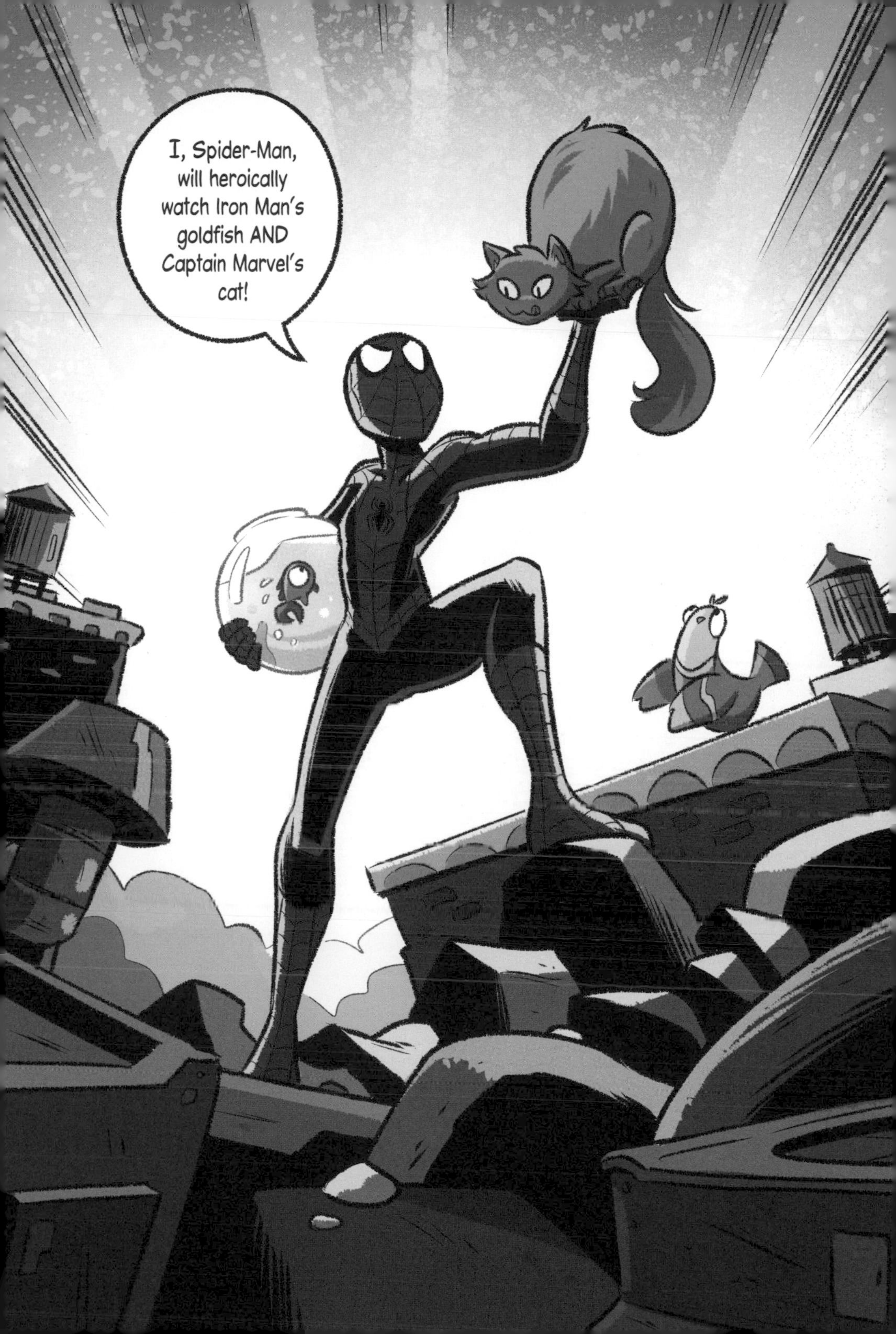
I, Spider-Man, will heroically watch Iron Man's goldfish AND Captain Marvel's cat!

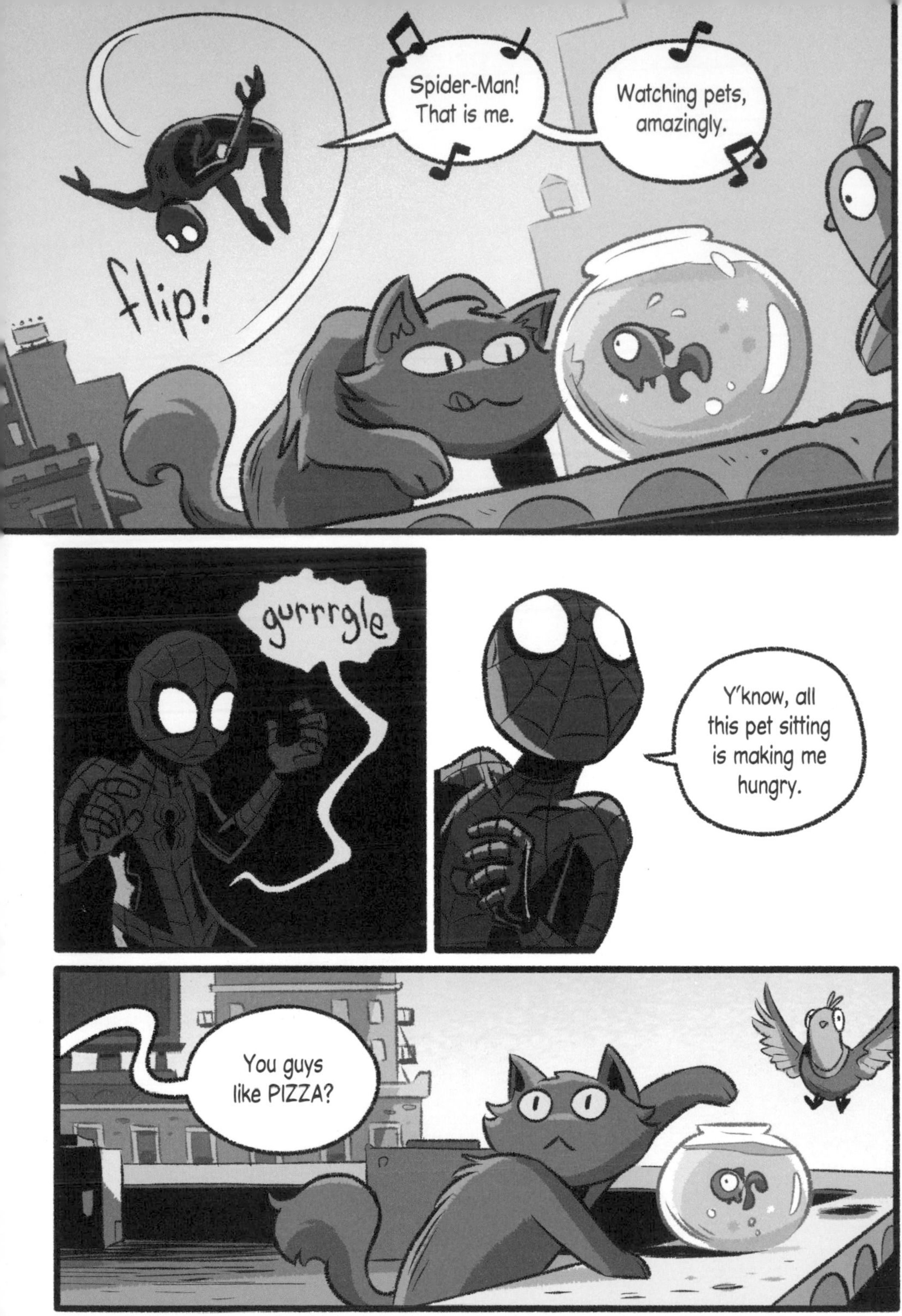
Spider-Man! That is me.
Watching pets, amazingly.
flip!
gurrrgle
Y'know, all this pet sitting is making me hungry.
You guys like PIZZA?

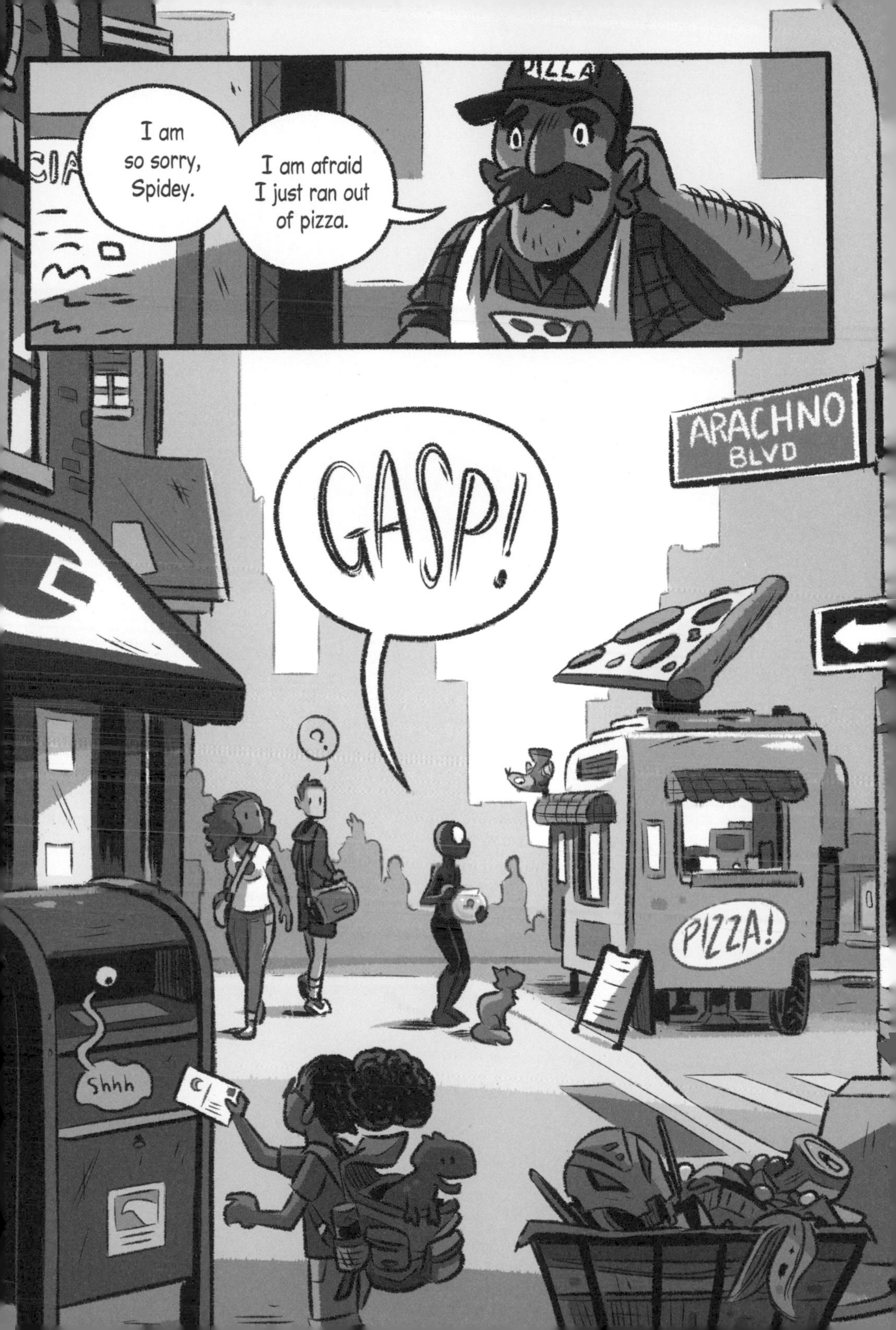

I am so sorry, Spidey.
I am afraid I just ran out of pizza.
ARACHNO BLVD
GASP!
?
PIZZA!
Shhh

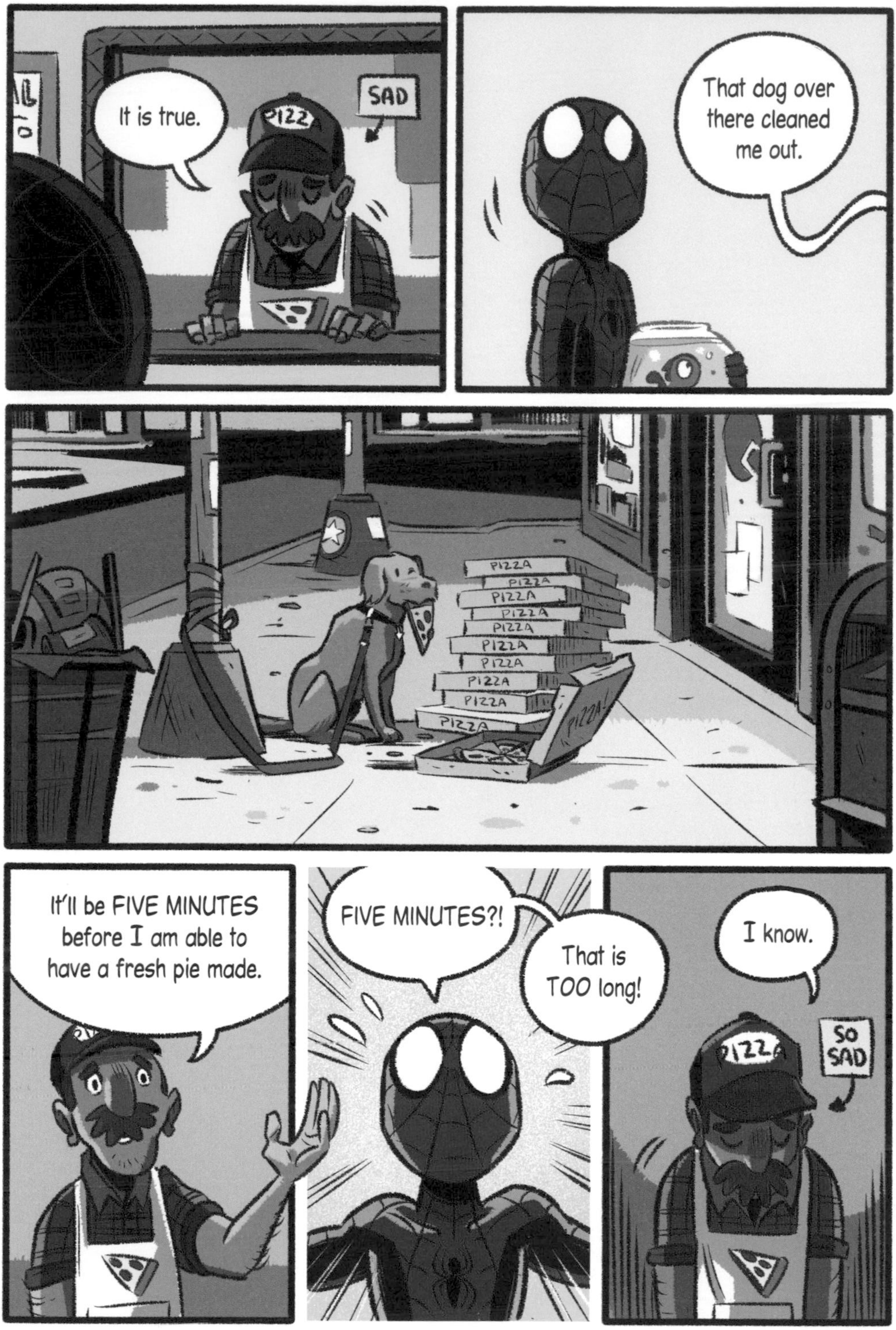
It is true.
SAD
PIZZA
That dog over there cleaned me out.
PIZZA
PIZZA
PIZZA
PIZZA
PIZZA
PIZZA
PIZZA
PIZZA
PIZZA
PIZZA
PIZZA!
It'll be FIVE MINUTES before I am able to have a fresh pie made.
FIVE MINUTES?!
That is TOO long!
I know.
SO SAD

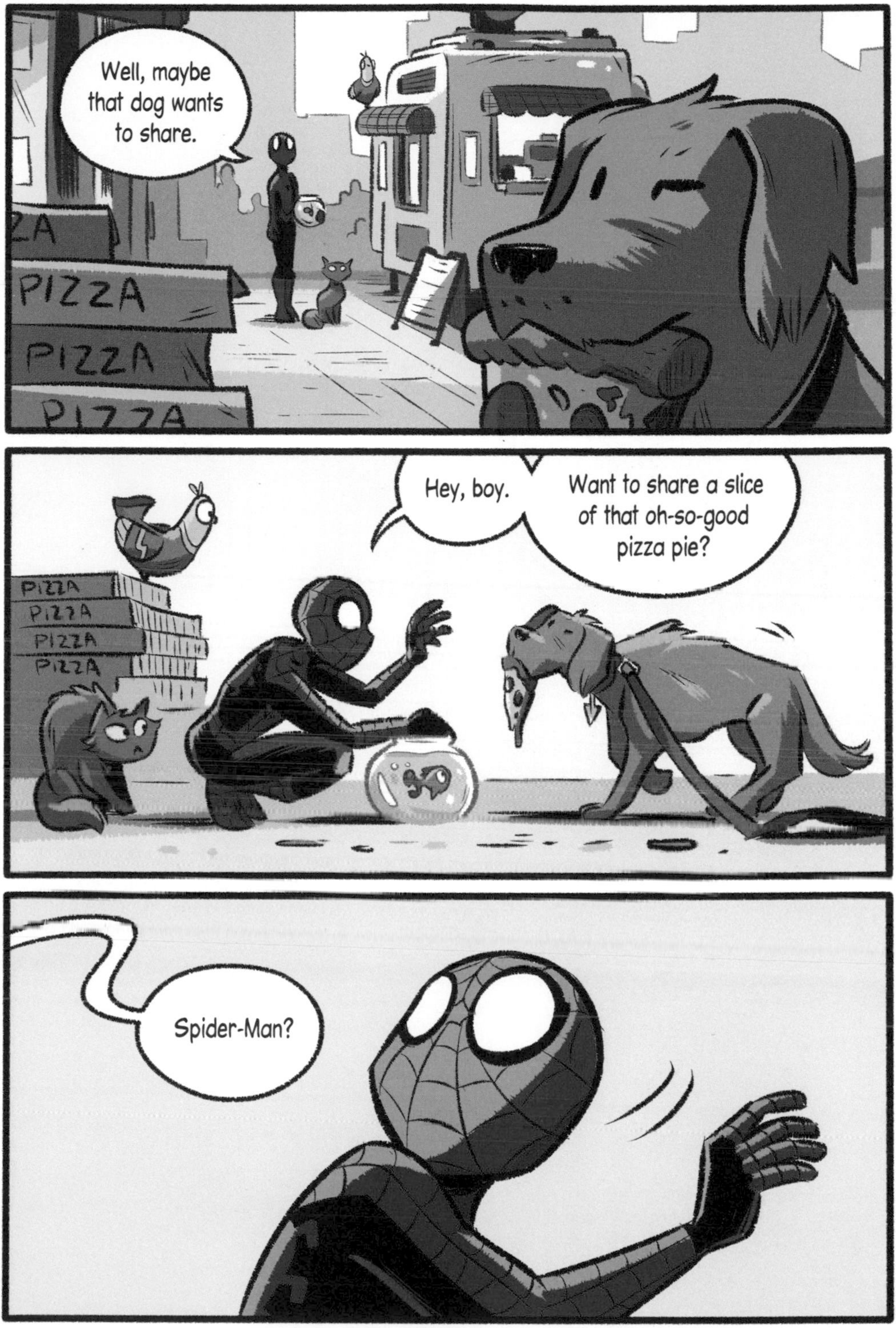
Well, maybe that dog wants to share.
PIZZA
PIZZA
PIZZA
Hey, boy.
Want to share a slice of that oh-so-good pizza pie?
PIZZA
PIZZA
PIZZA
PIZZA
Spider-Man?

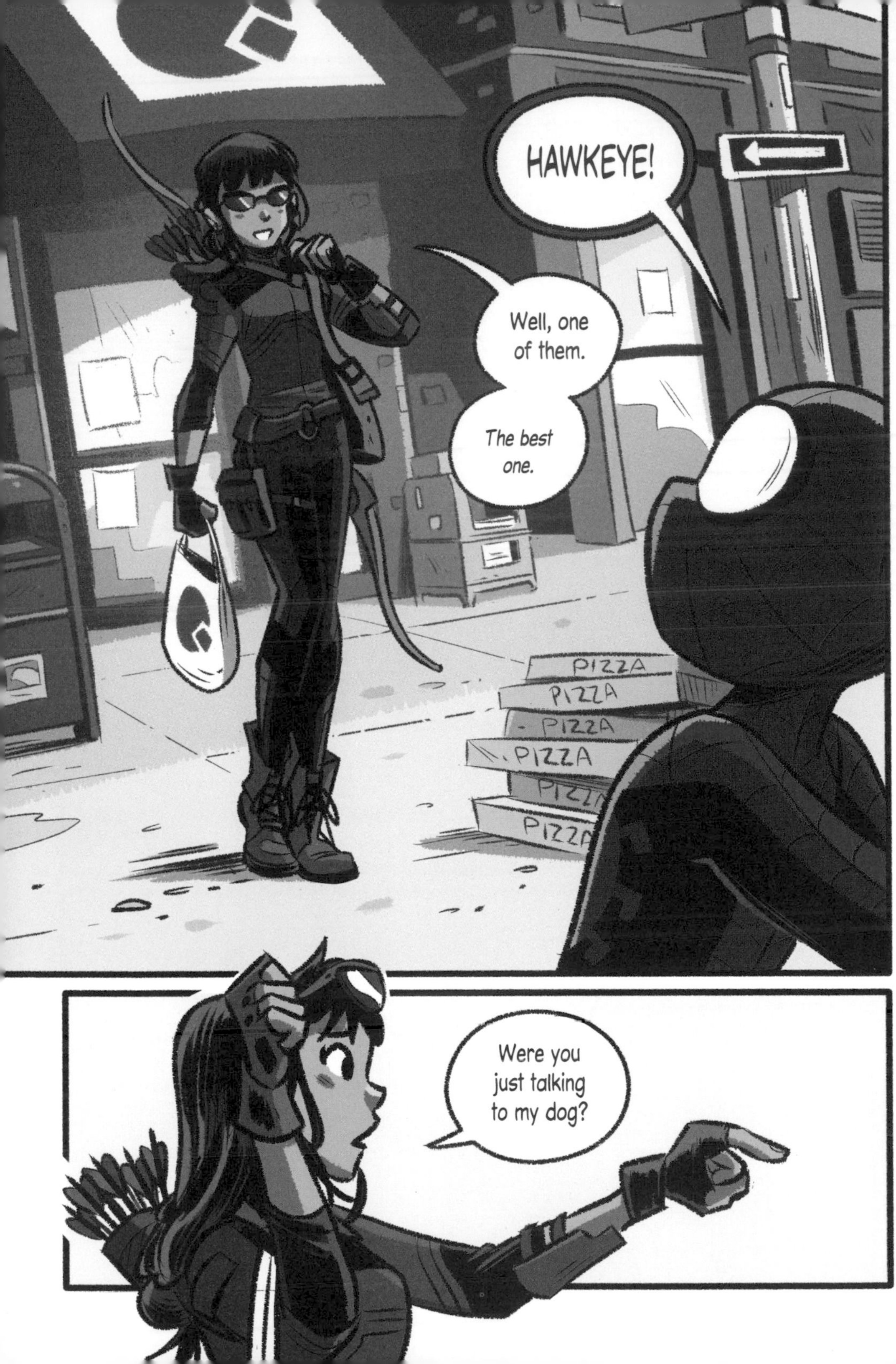
HAWKEYE!
Well, one of them.
The best one.
PIZZA
PIZZA
PIZZA
PIZZA
PIZZA
Were you just talking to my dog?

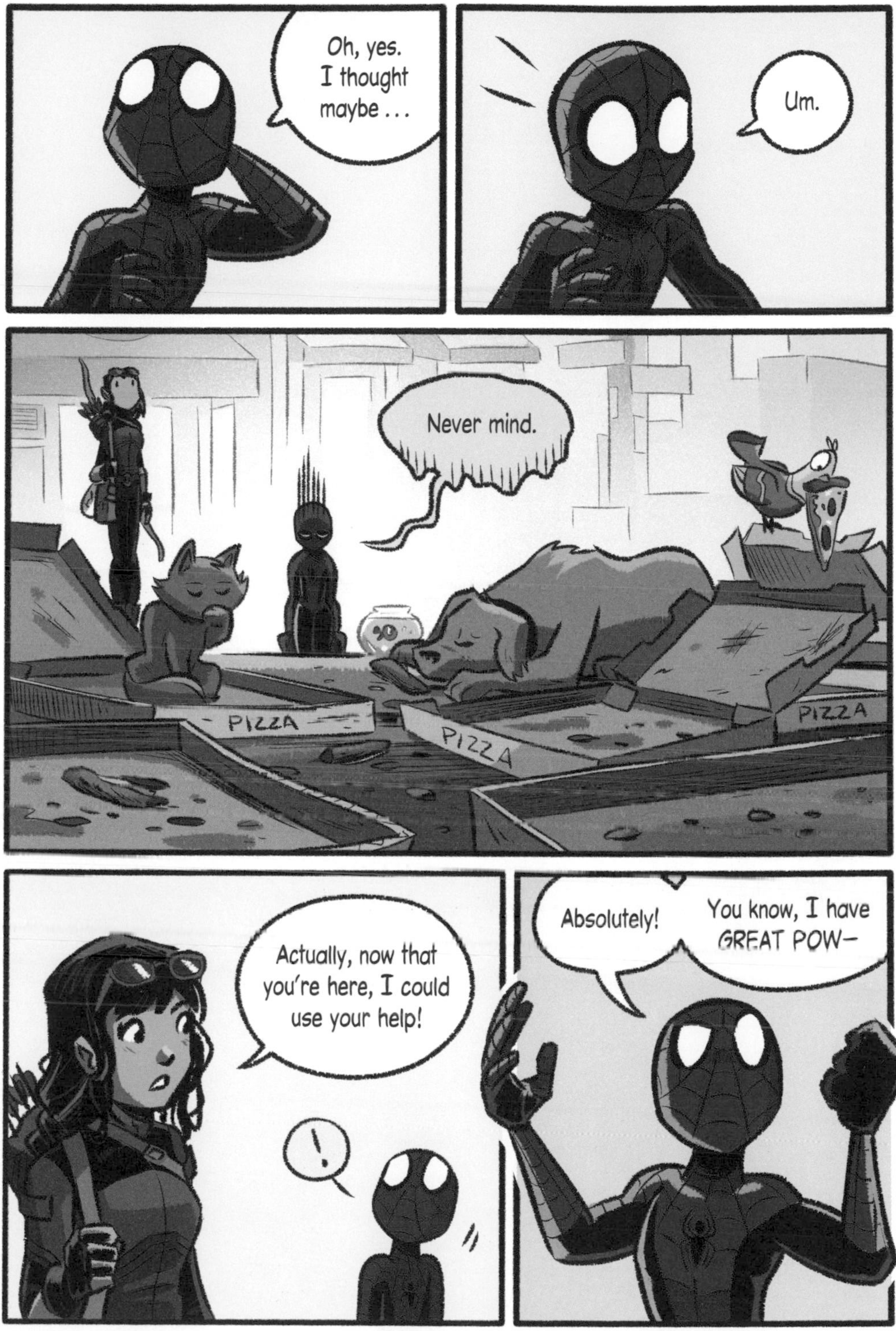
Oh, yes. I thought maybe . . .
Um.
Never mind.
PIZZA
PIZZA
PIZZA
Actually, now that you're here, I could use your help!
!
Absolutely!
You know, I have GREAT POW–

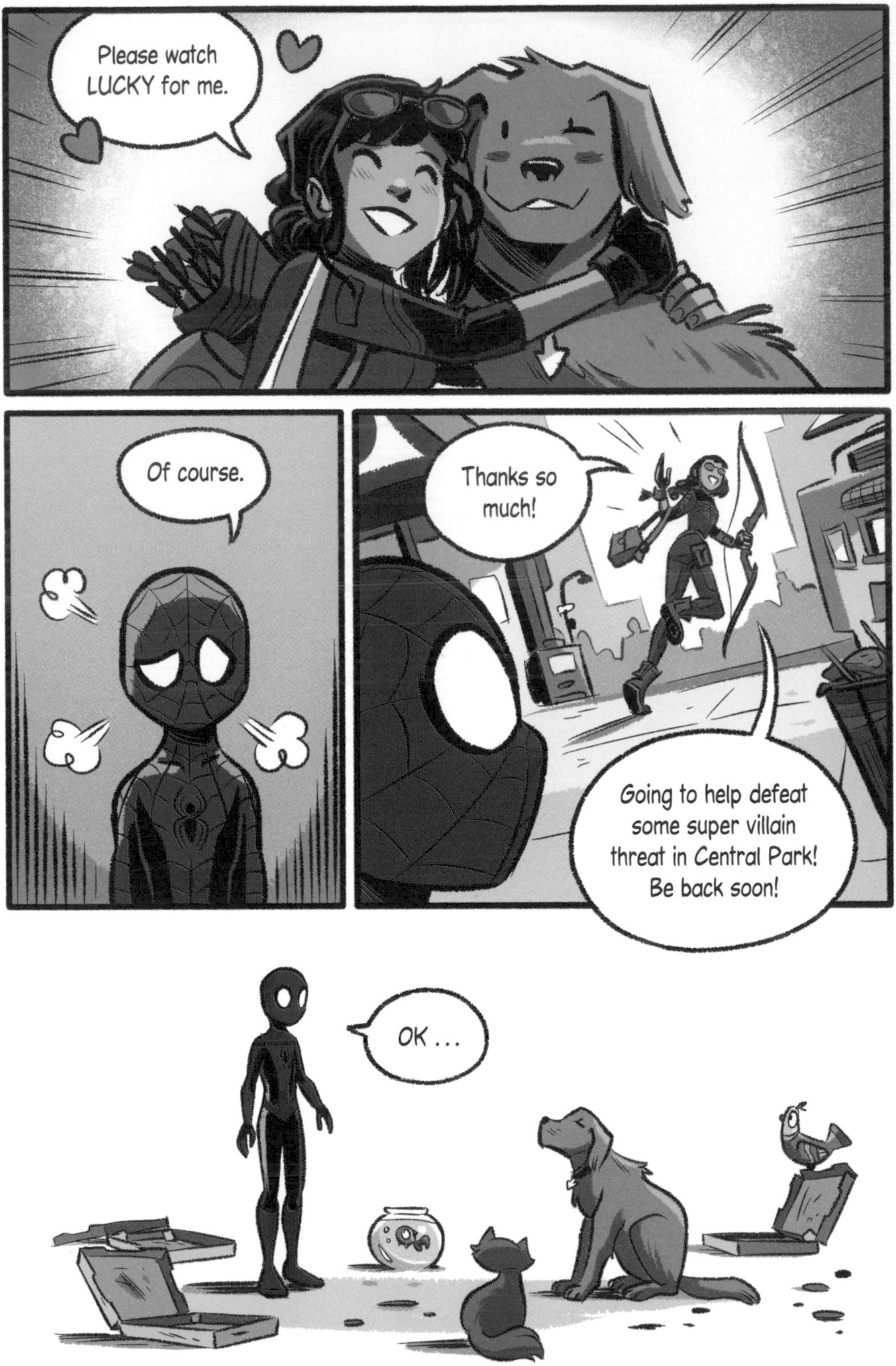
Please watch LUCKY for me.
Of course.
Thanks so much!
Going to help defeat some super villain threat in Central Park! Be back soon!
OK . . .

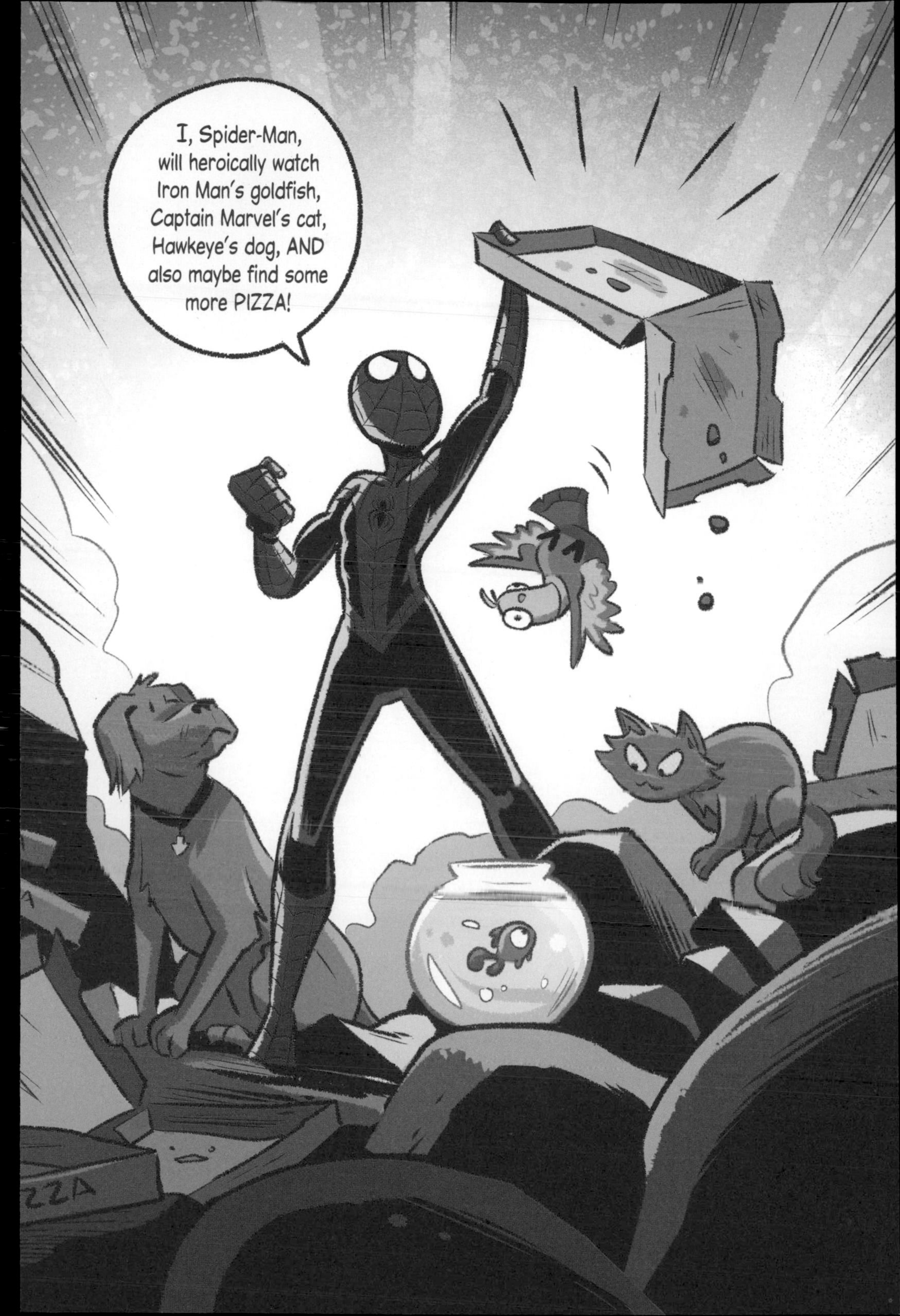
I, Spider-Man, will heroically watch Iron Man's goldfish, Captain Marvel's cat, Hawkeye's dog, AND also maybe find some more PIZZA!
PIZZA

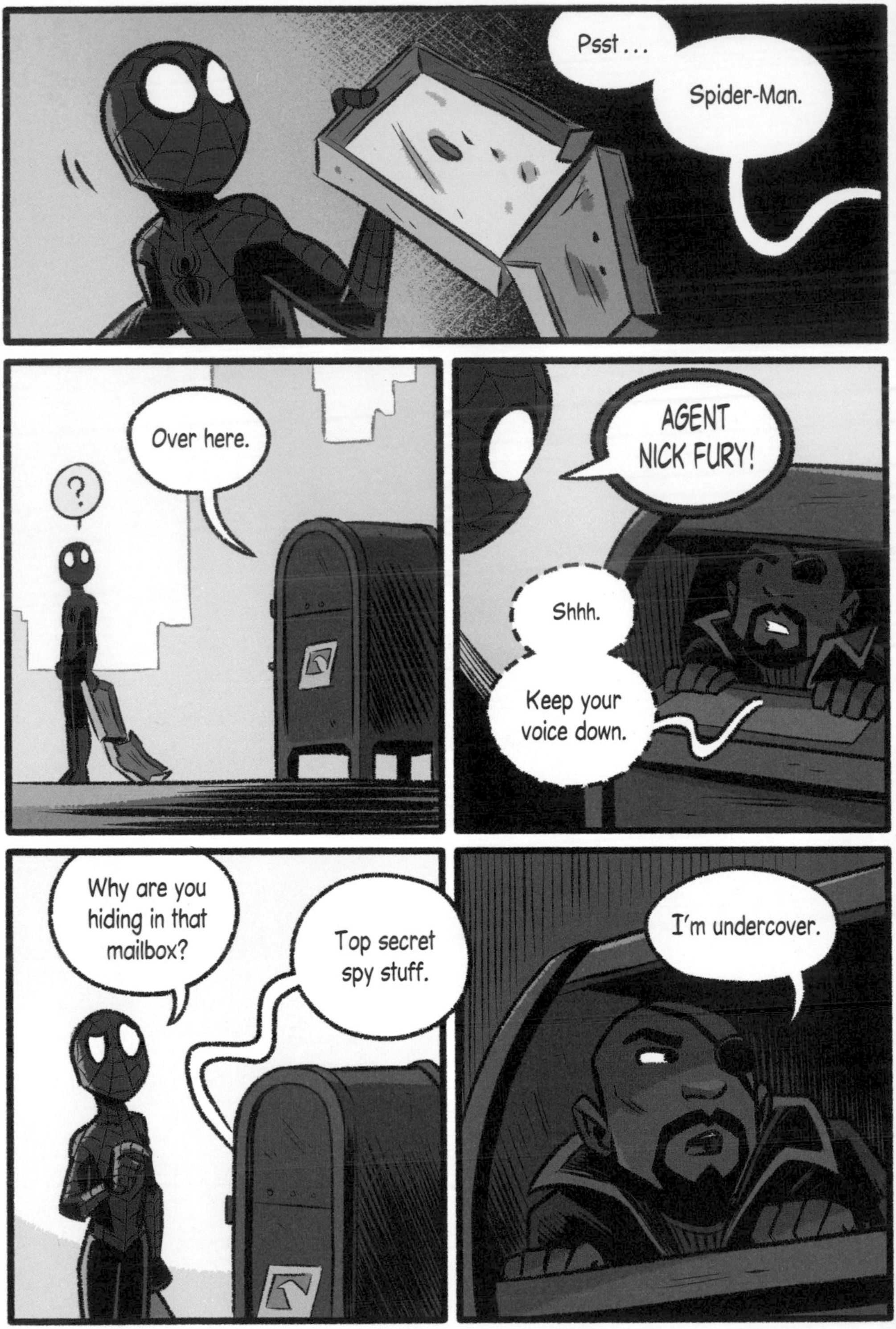
Psst . . .
Spider-Man.
Over here.
?
AGENT NICK FURY!
Shhh.
Keep your voice down.
Why are you hiding in that mailbox?
Top secret spy stuff.
I'm undercover.

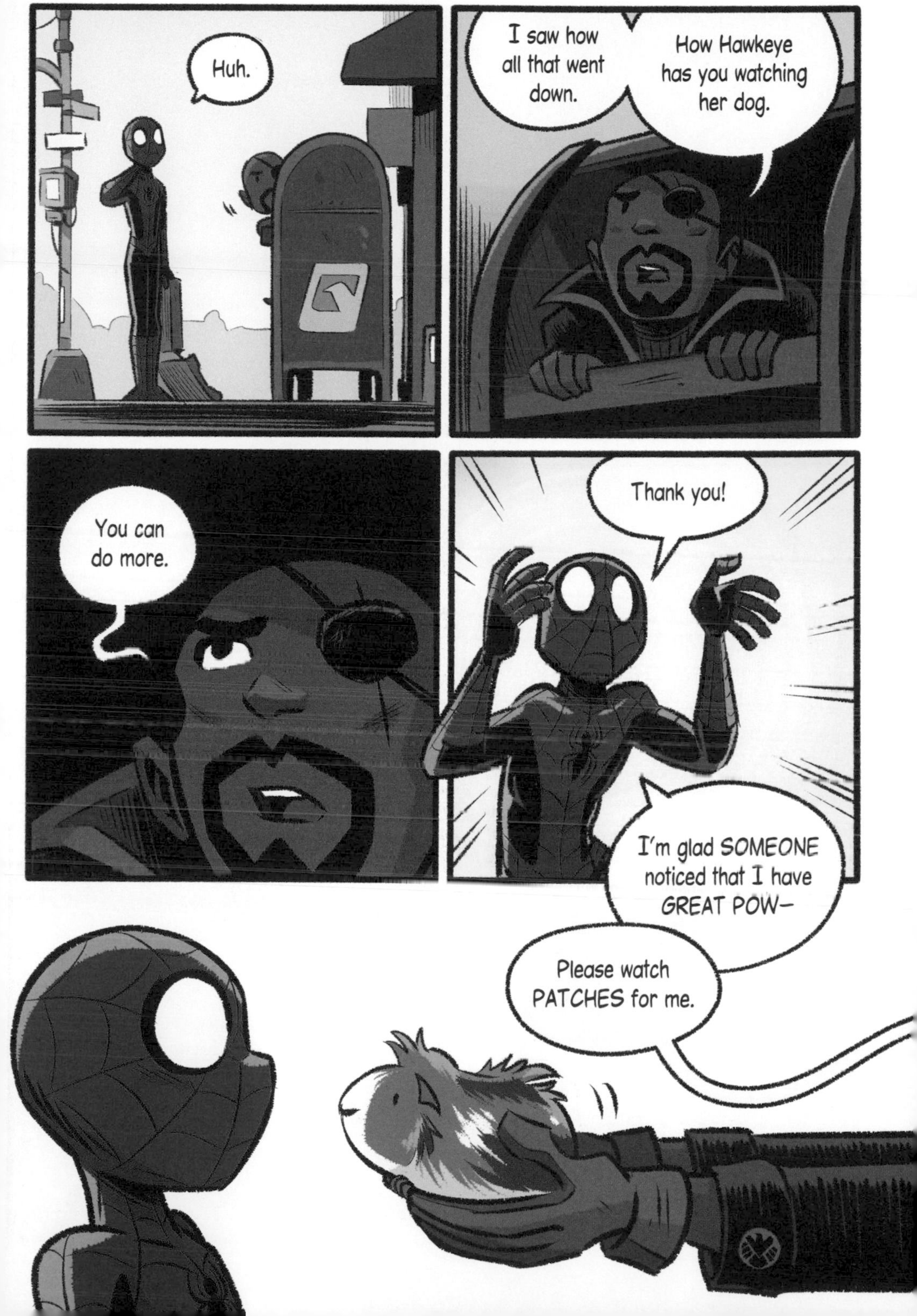
Huh.
I saw how all that went down.
How Hawkeye has you watching her dog.
You can do more.
Thank you!
I'm glad SOMEONE noticed that I have GREAT POW—
Please watch PATCHES for me.

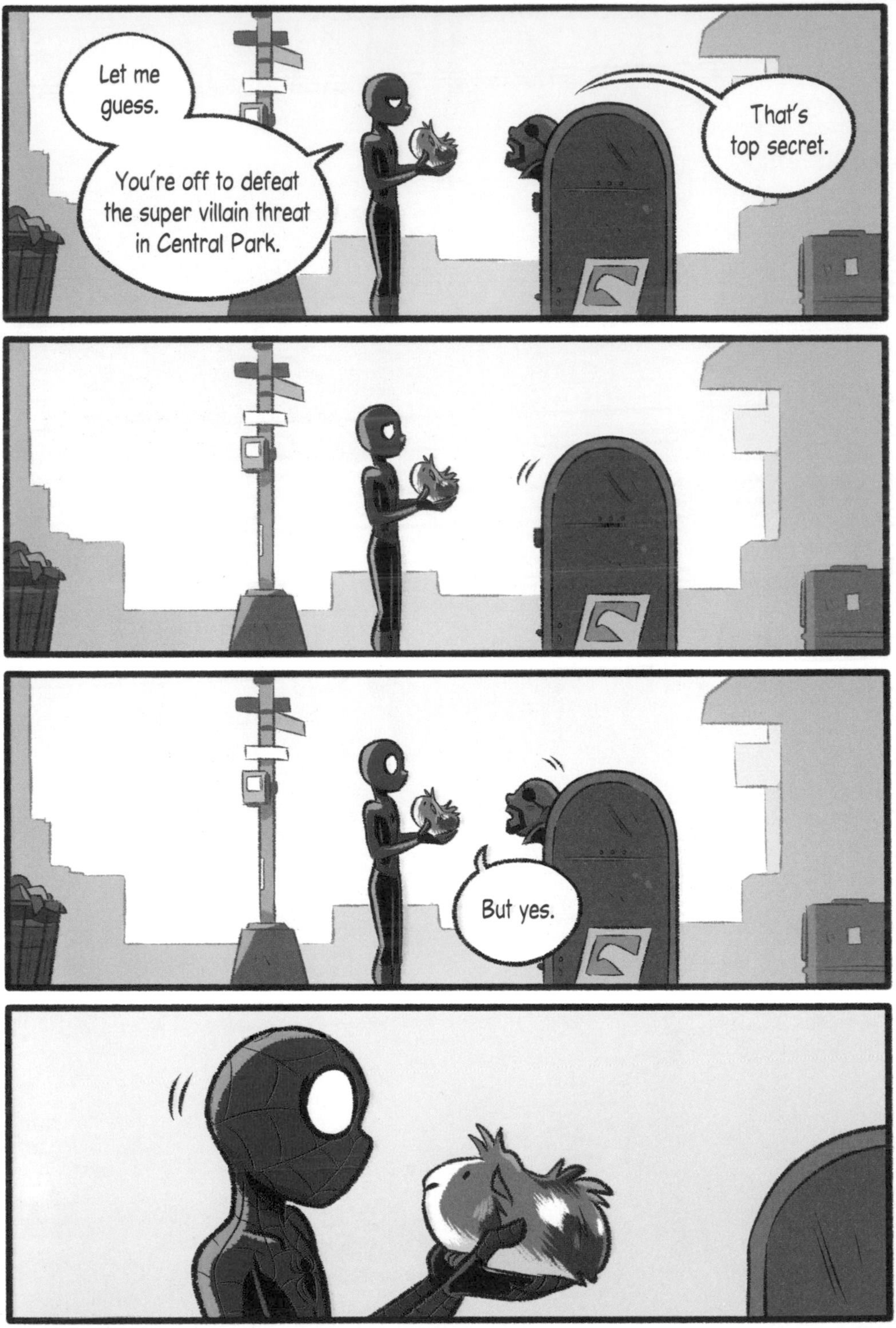
Let me guess.
You're off to defeat the super villain threat in Central Park.
That's top secret.
But yes.

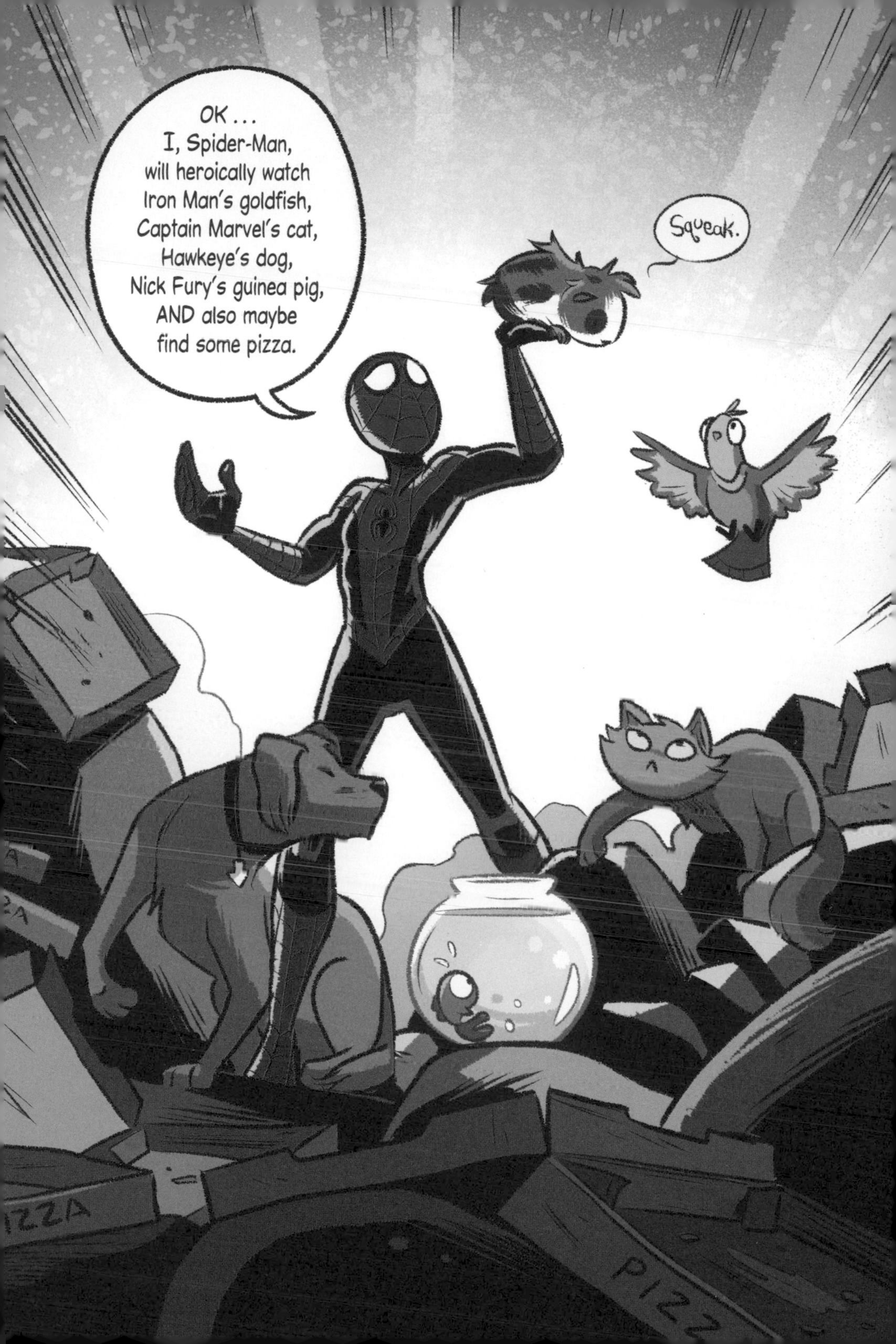
OK . . . I, Spider-Man, will heroically watch Iron Man's goldfish, Captain Marvel's cat, Hawkeye's dog, Nick Fury's guinea pig, AND also maybe find some pizza.
Squeak.

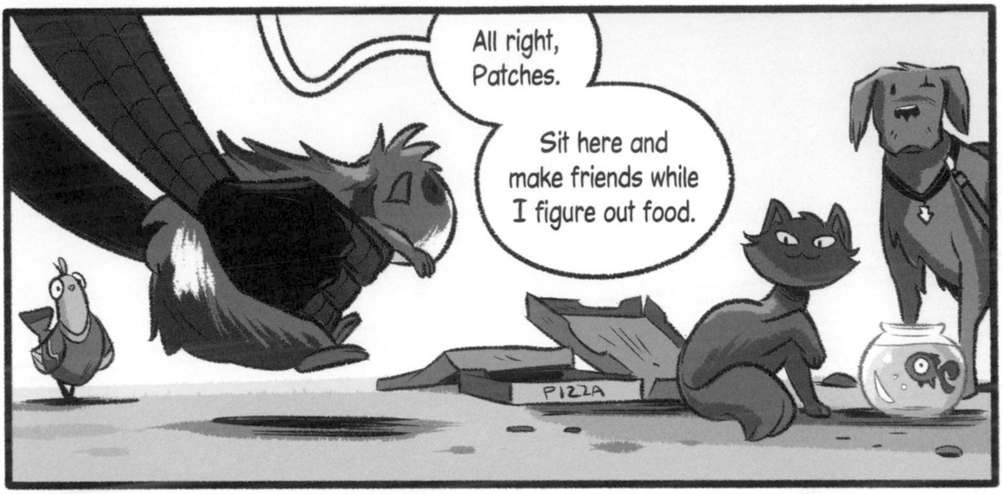
All right, Patches.
Sit here and make friends while I figure out food.
PIZZA

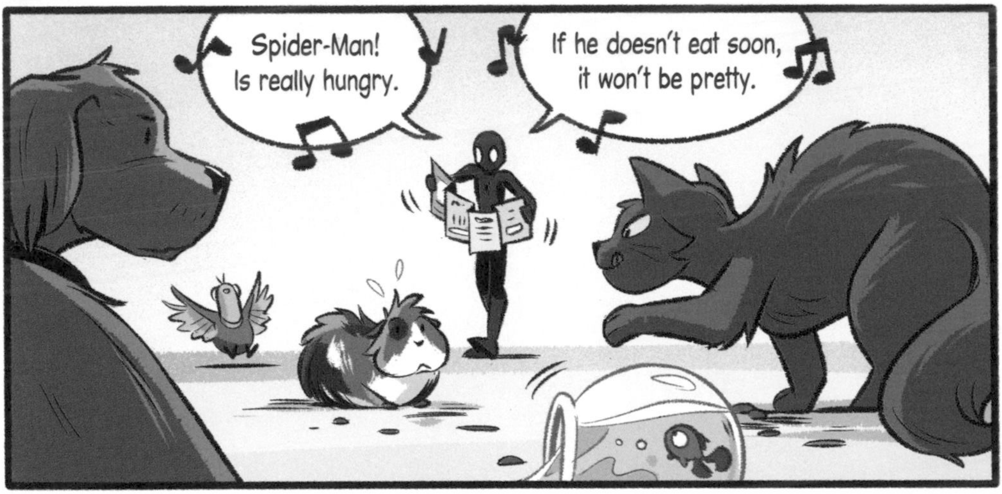
Spider-Man! Is really hungry.
If he doesn't eat soon, it won't be pretty.

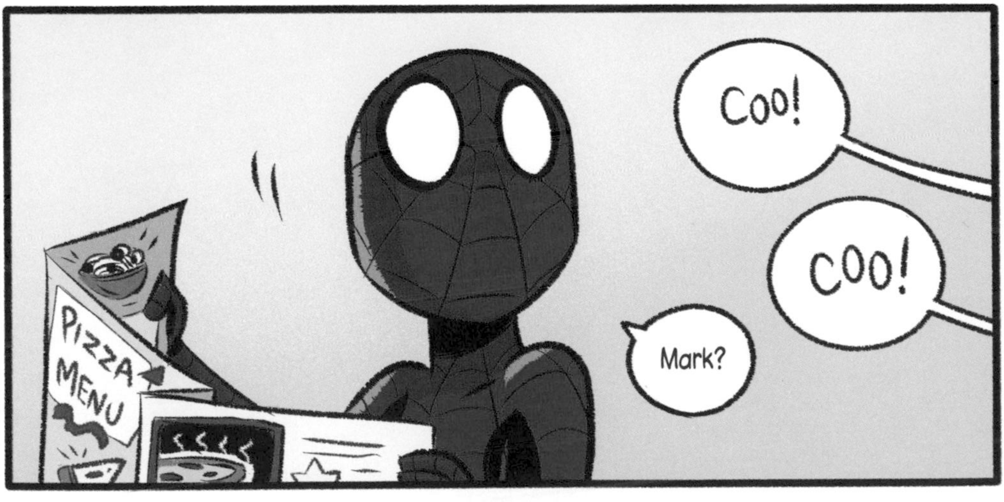
COO!
COO!
Mark?
PIZZA MENU

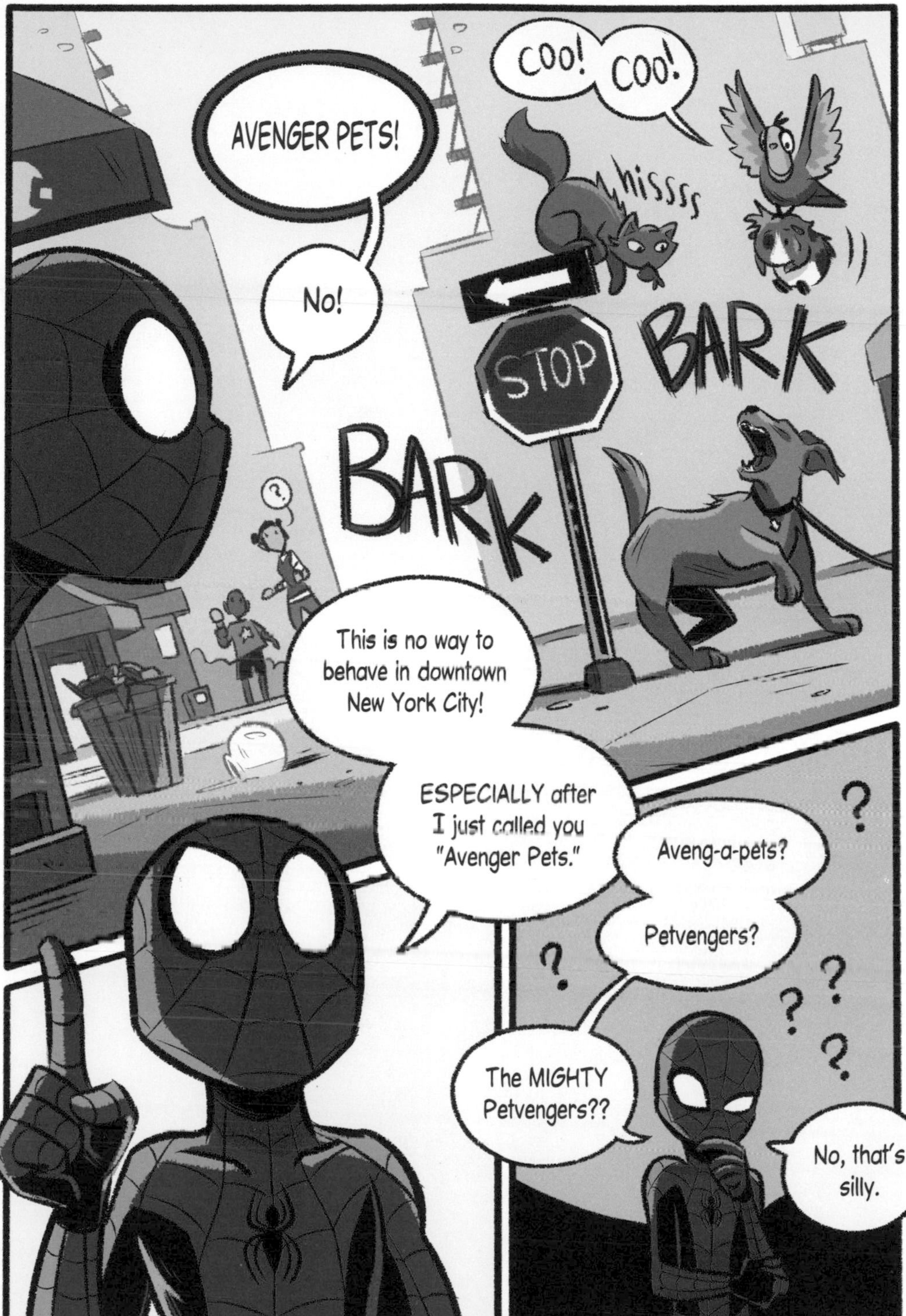
AVENGER PETS!
No!
COO! COO!
hissss
BARK
BARK
This is no way to behave in downtown New York City!
ESPECIALLY after I just called you "Avenger Pets."
Aveng-a-pets?
Petvengers?
The MIGHTY Petvengers??
No, that's silly.

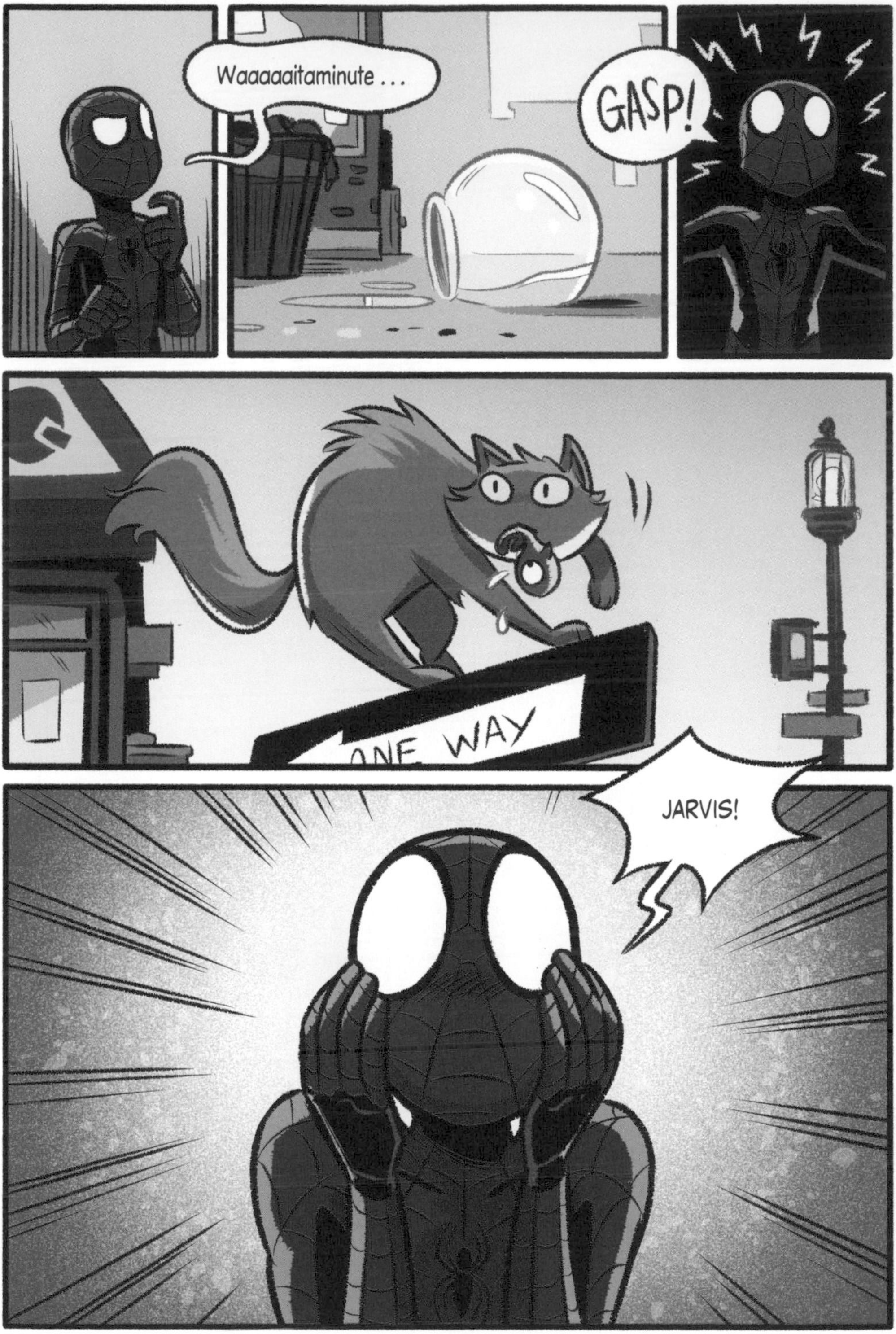
Waaaaaitaminute . . .
GASP!
ONE WAY
JARVIS!

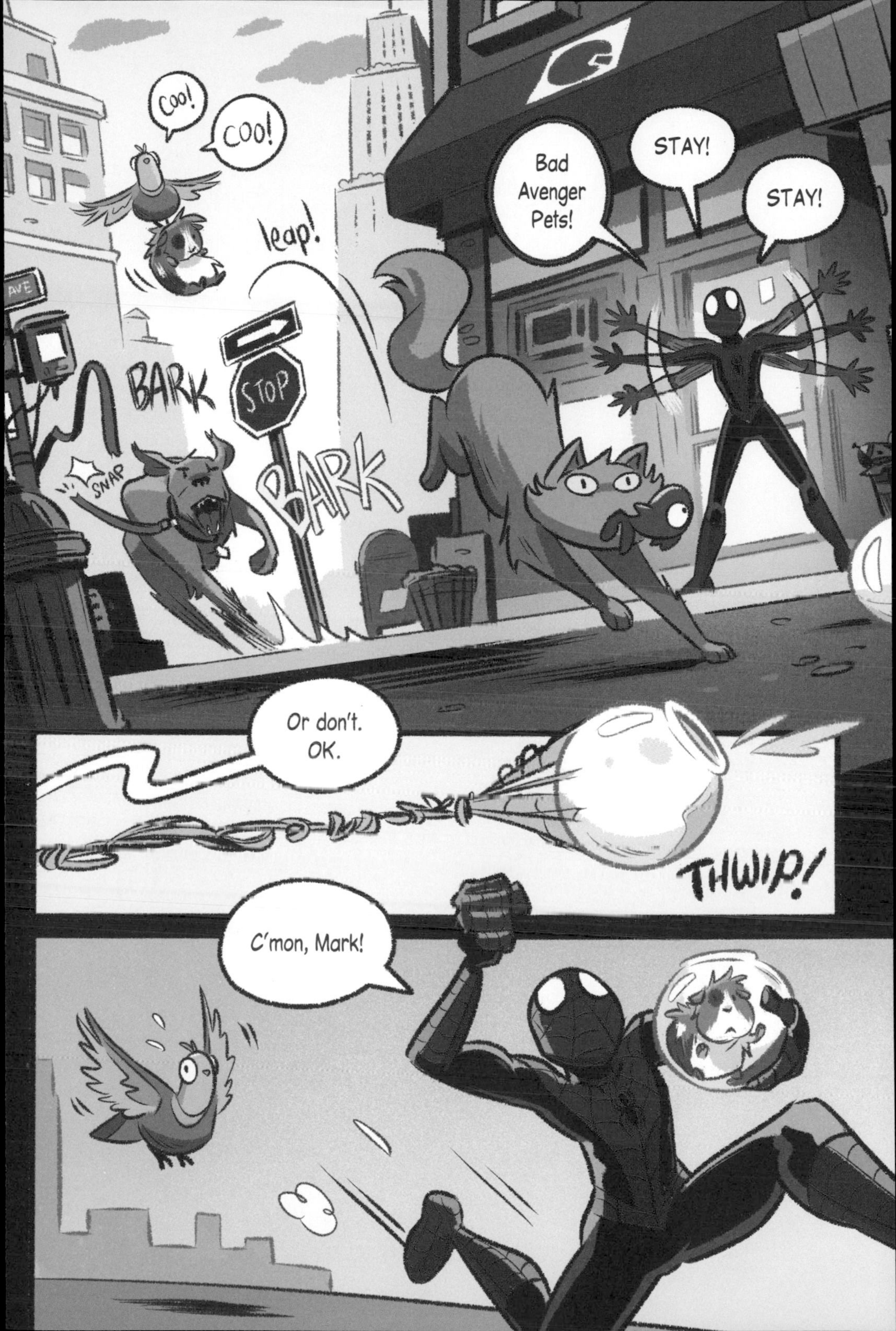
COO!
COO!
leap!
AVE
BARK
STOP
SNAP
BARK
Bad Avenger Pets!
STAY!
STAY!
Or don't. OK.
THWIP!
C'mon, Mark!

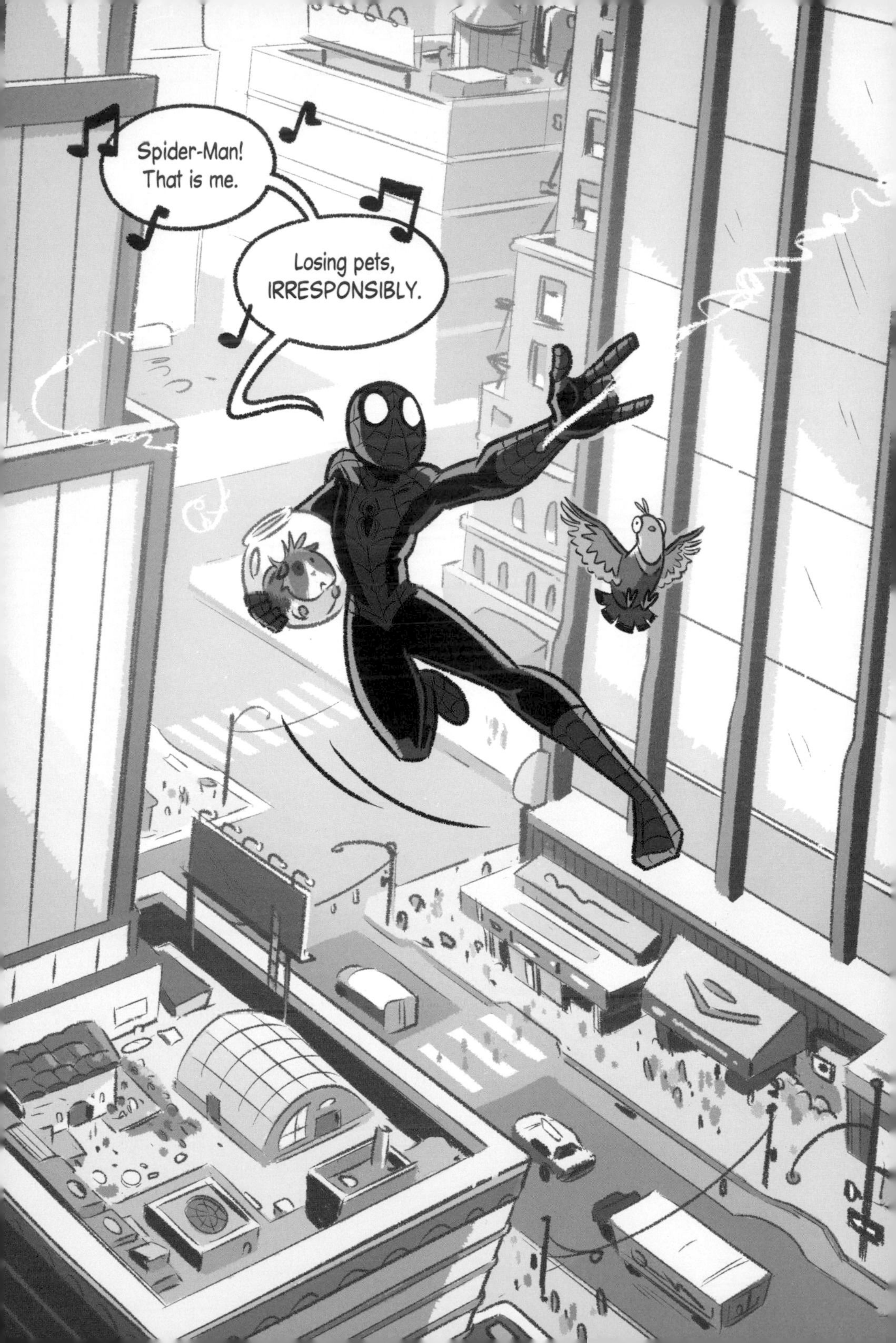
Spider-Man!
That is me.
Losing pets,
IRRESPONSIBLY.

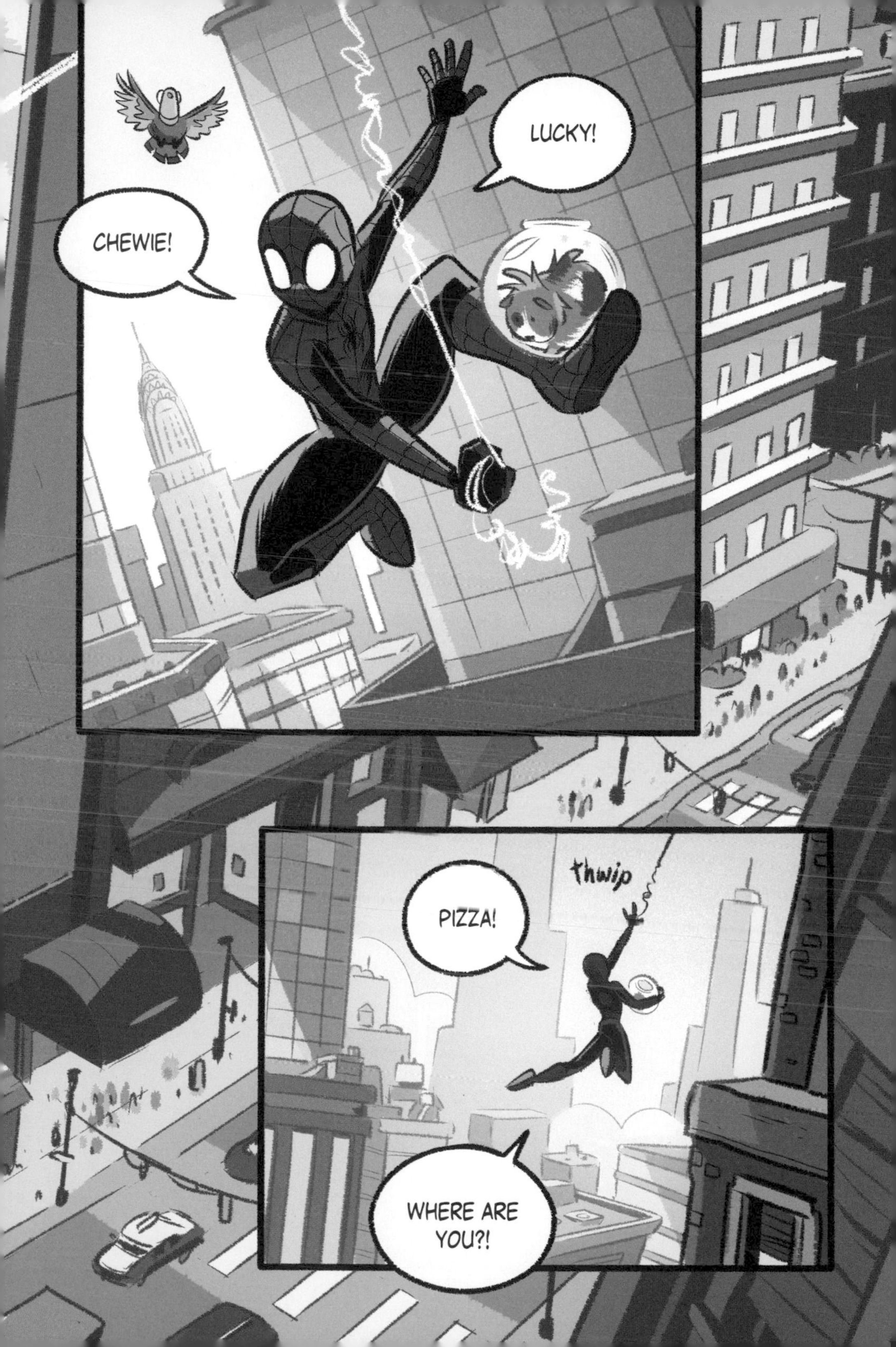
CHEWIE!
LUCKY!
PIZZA!
thwip
WHERE ARE YOU?!

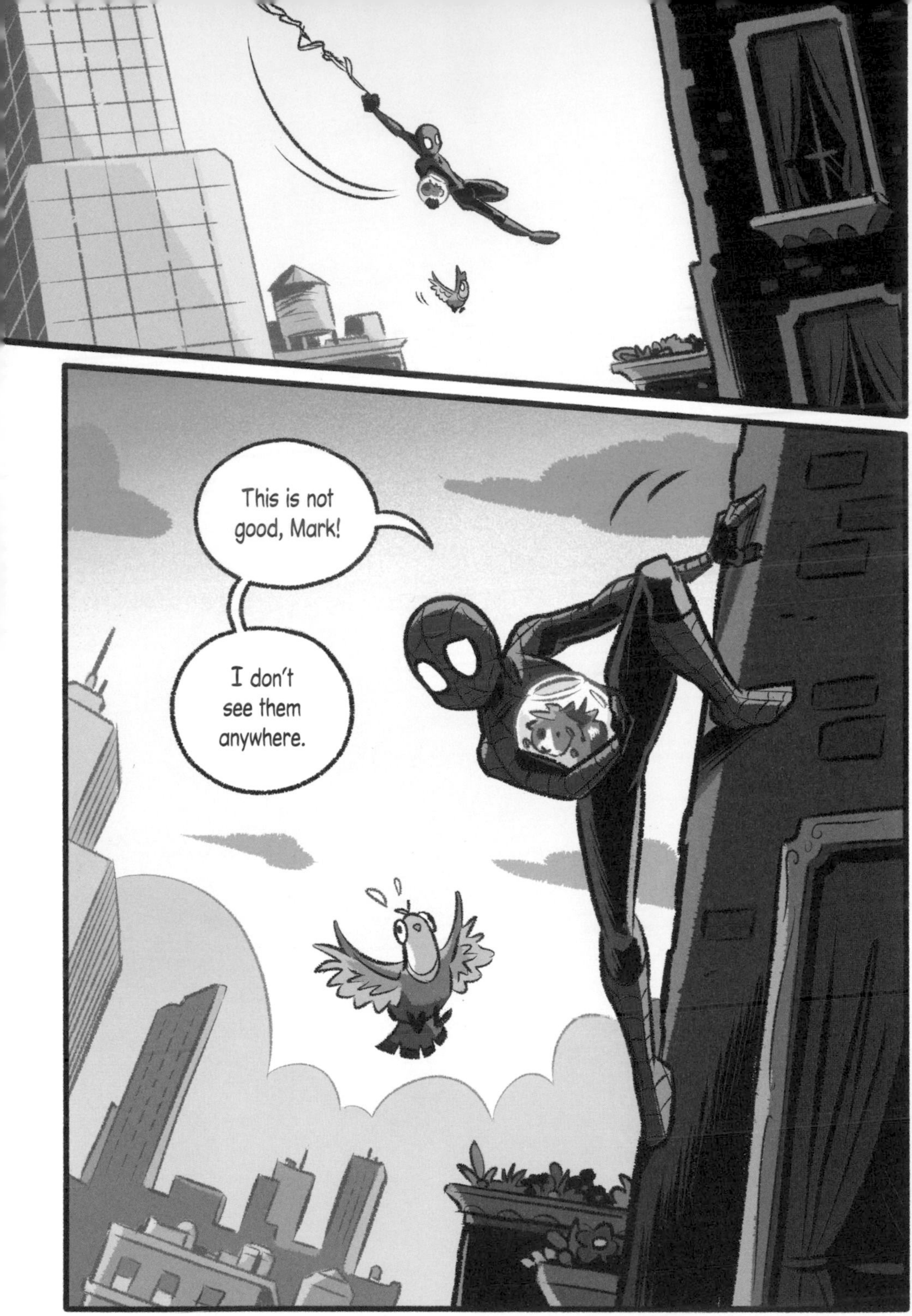
This is not good, Mark!
I don't see them anywhere.

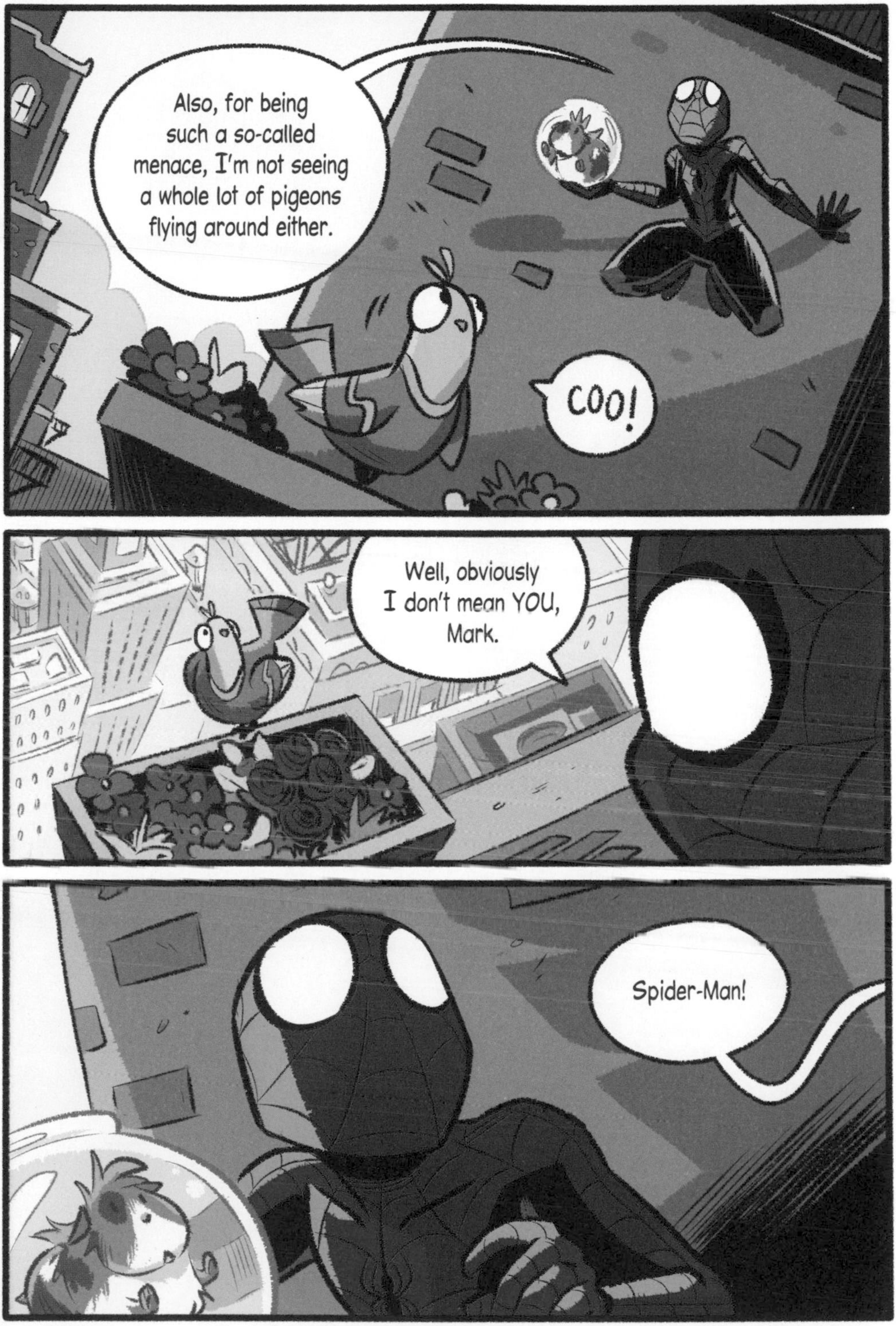
Also, for being such a so-called menace, I'm not seeing a whole lot of pigeons flying around either.
COO!
Well, obviously I don't mean YOU, Mark.
Spider-Man!

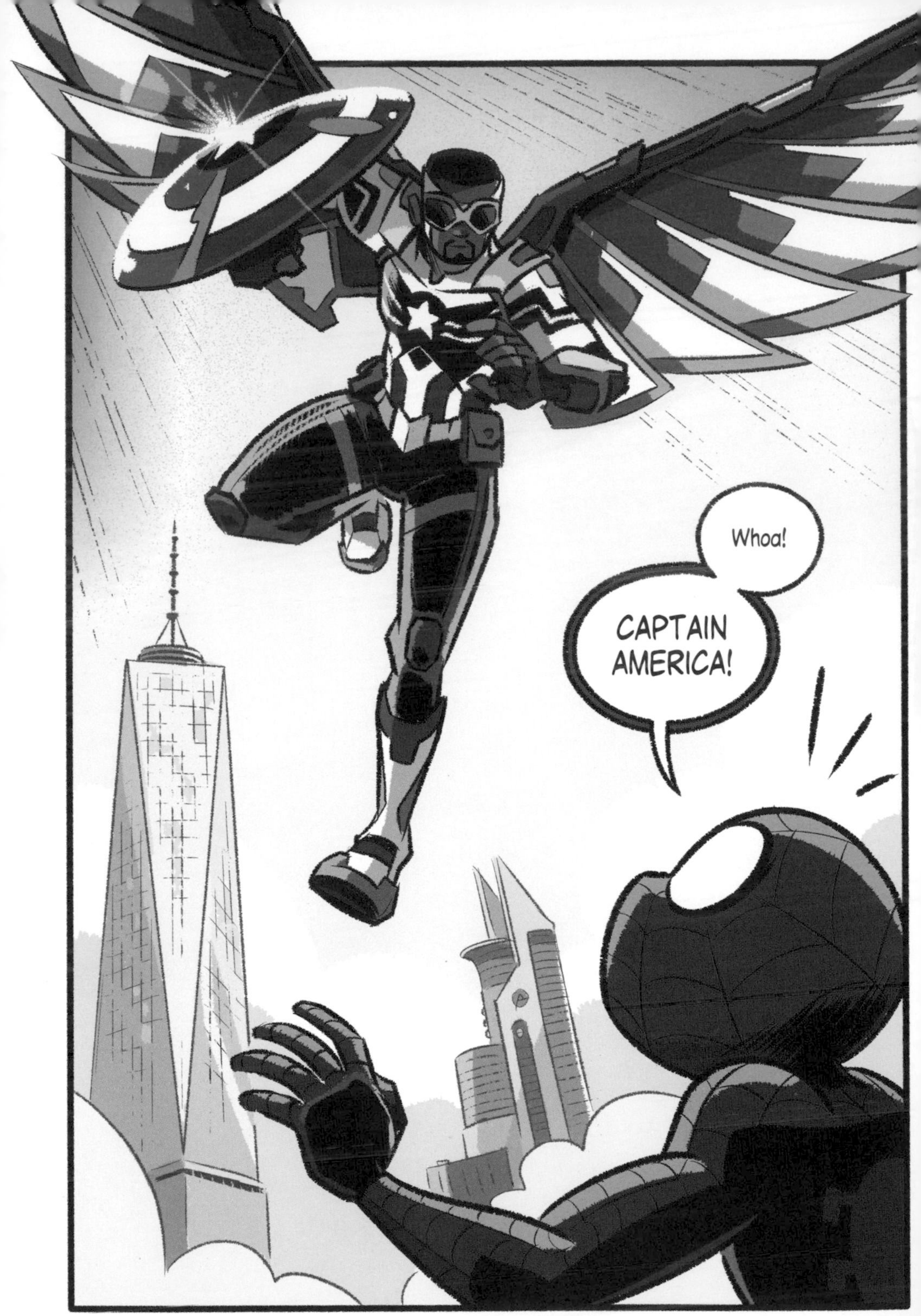
Whoa!
CAPTAIN AMERICA!

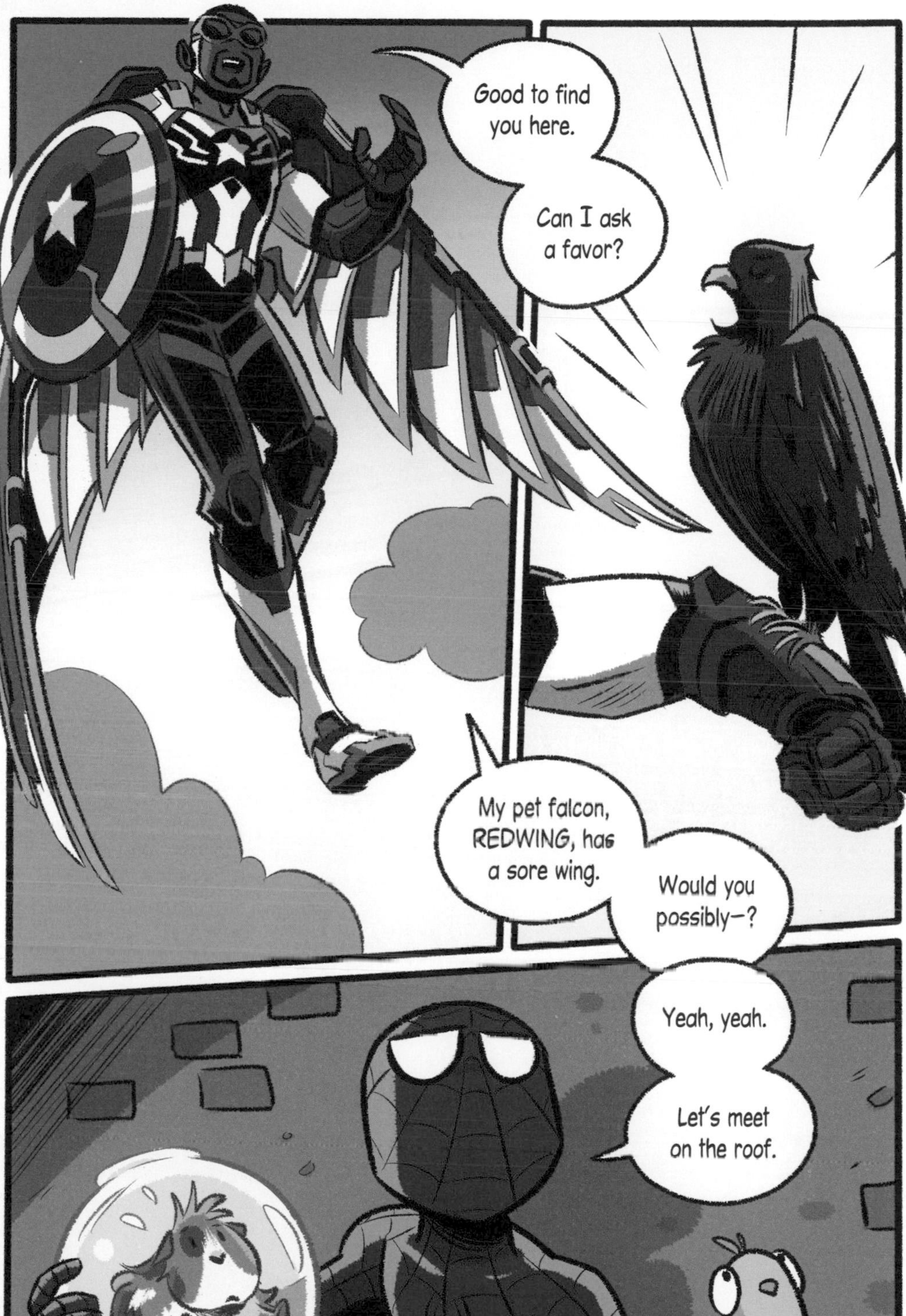
Good to find you here.
Can I ask a favor?
My pet falcon, REDWING, has a sore wing.
Would you possibly—?
Yeah, yeah.
Let's meet on the roof.

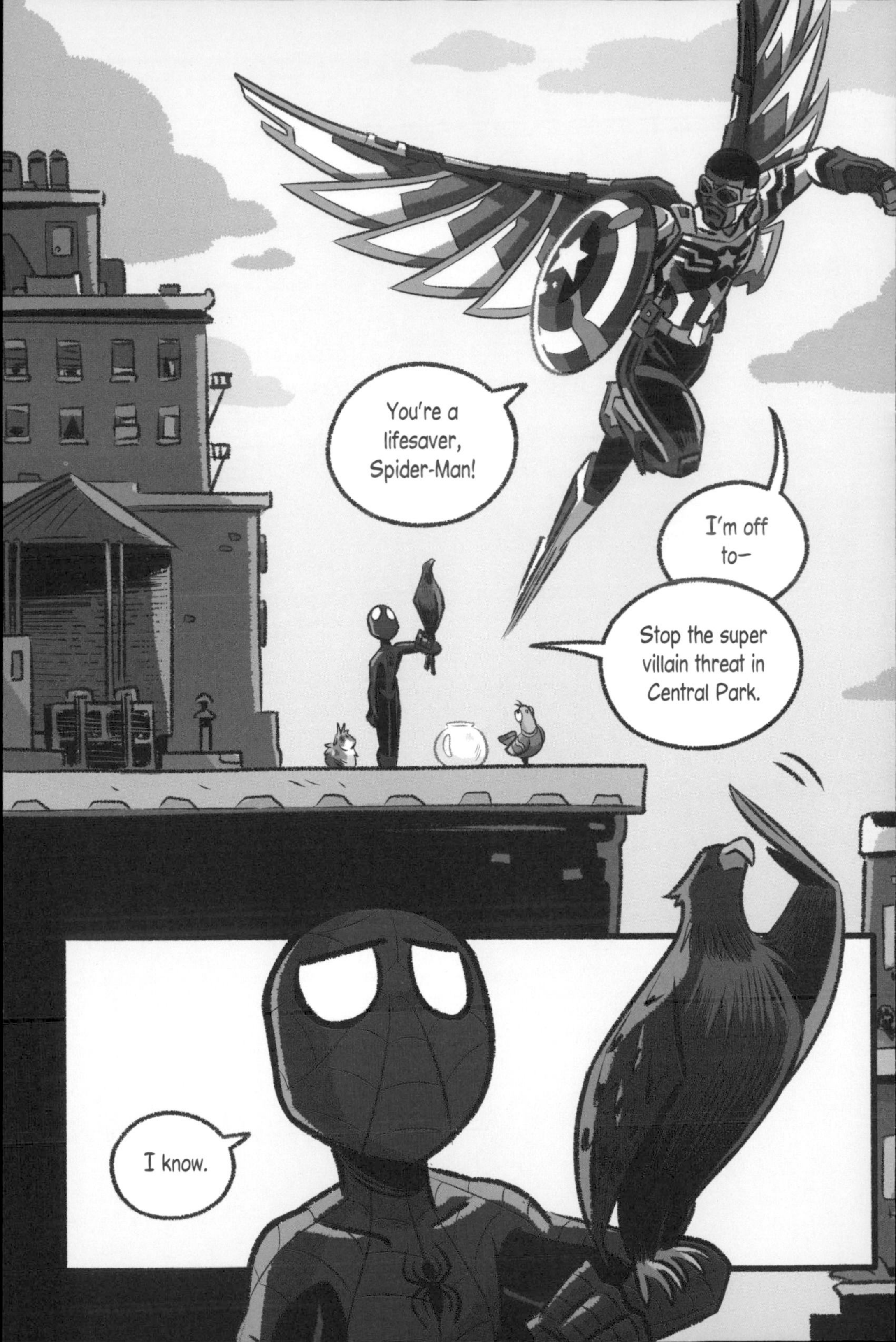
You're a lifesaver, Spider-Man!
I'm off to—
Stop the super villain threat in Central Park.
I know.

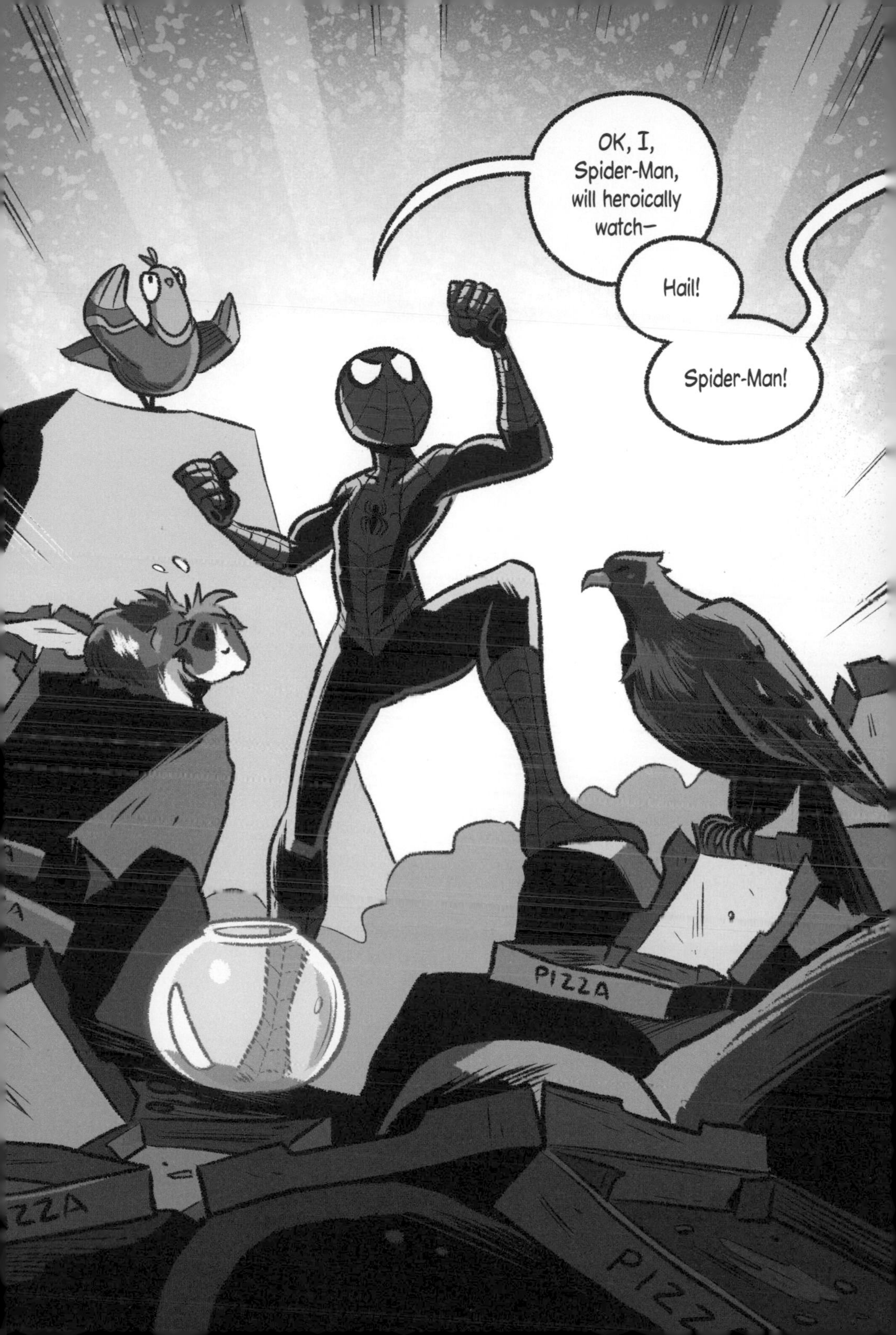
OK, I, Spider-Man, will heroically watch—
Hail!
Spider-Man!
PIZZA
ZZA
PIZZ

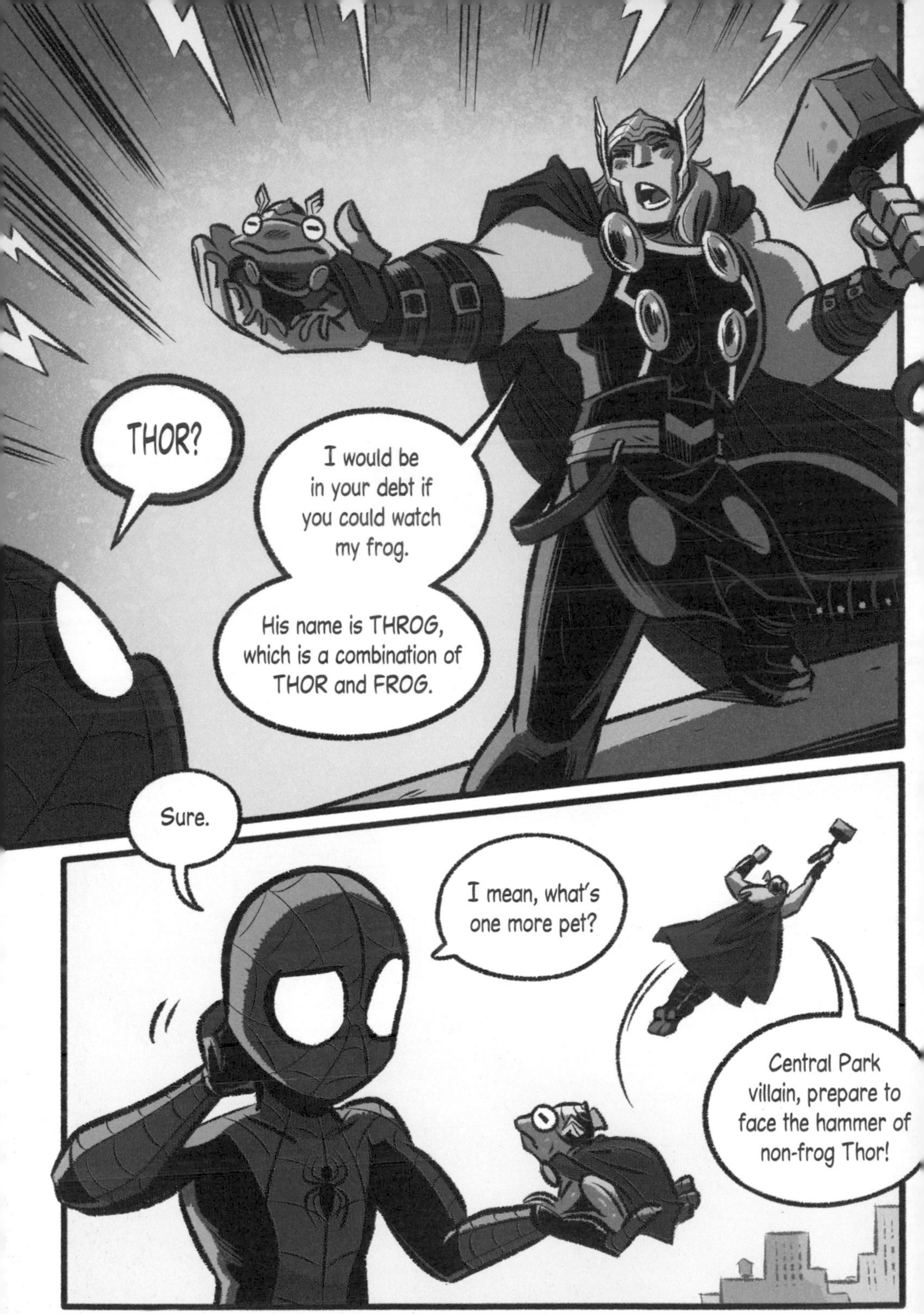
THOR?
I would be in your debt if you could watch my frog.
His name is THROG, which is a combination of THOR and FROG.
Sure.
I mean, what's one more pet?
Central Park villain, prepare to face the hammer of non-frog Thor!

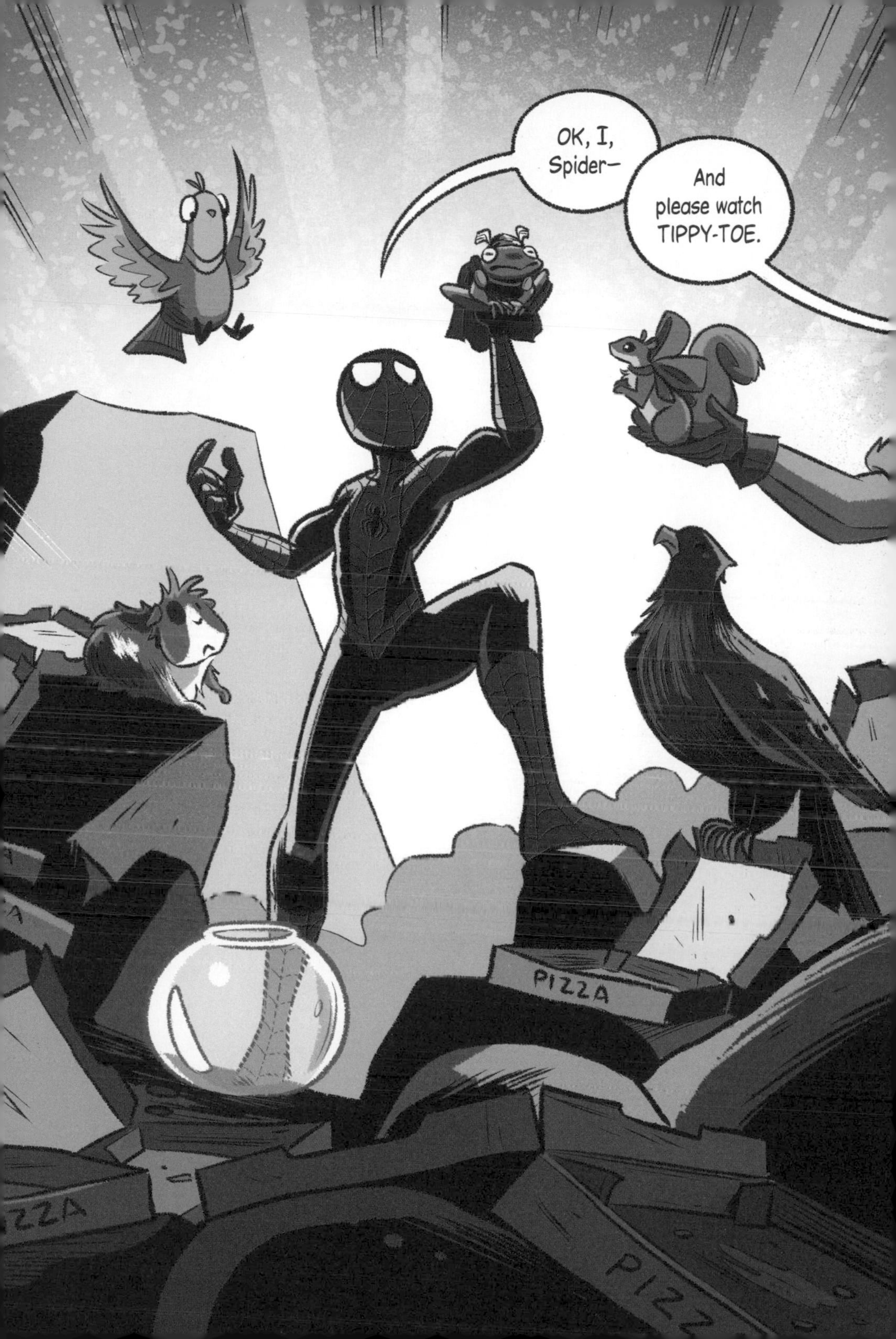
OK, I, Spider—
And please watch TIPPY-TOE.
PIZZA

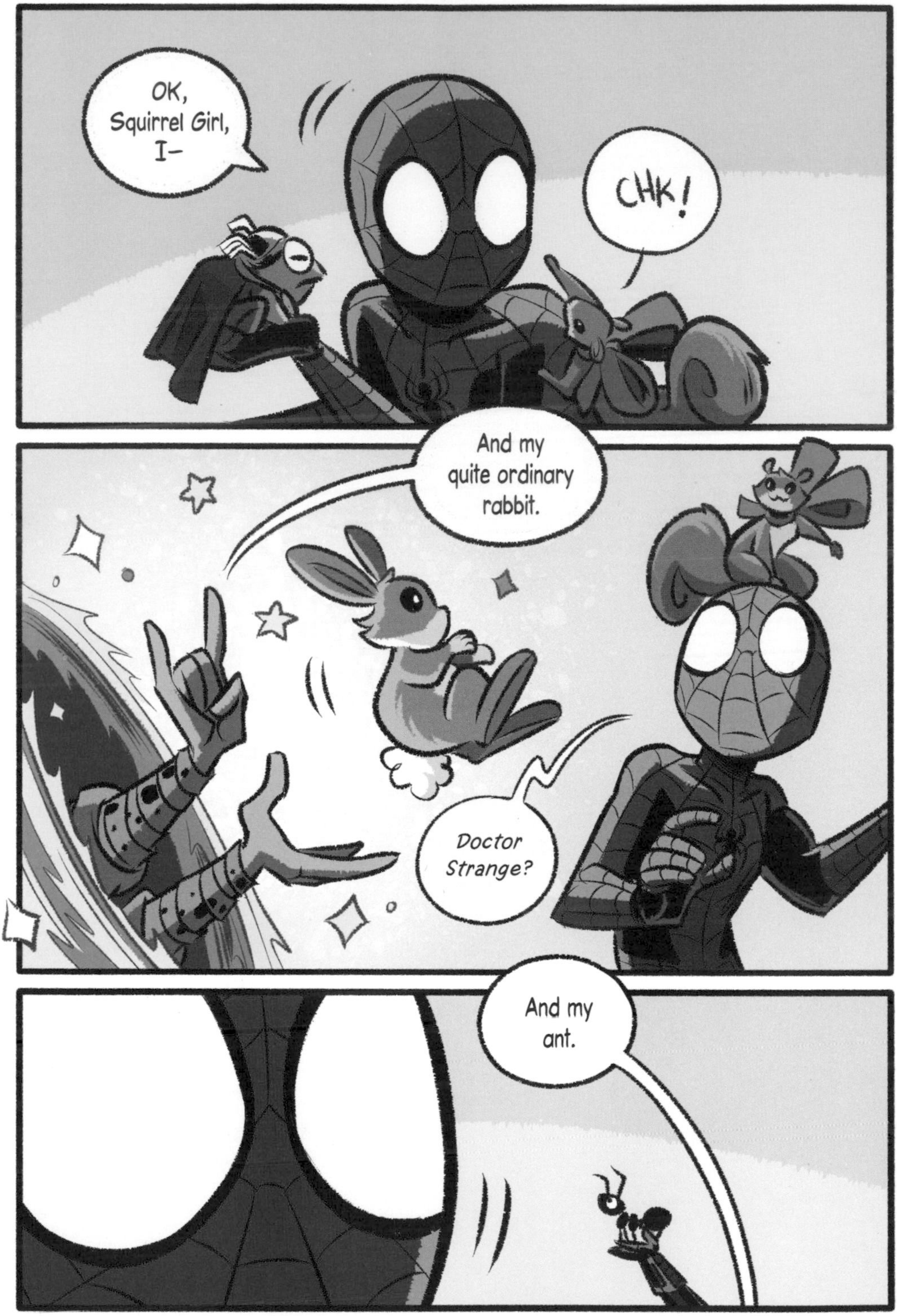
OK, Squirrel Girl, I–
CHK!
And my quite ordinary rabbit.
Doctor Strange?
And my ant.

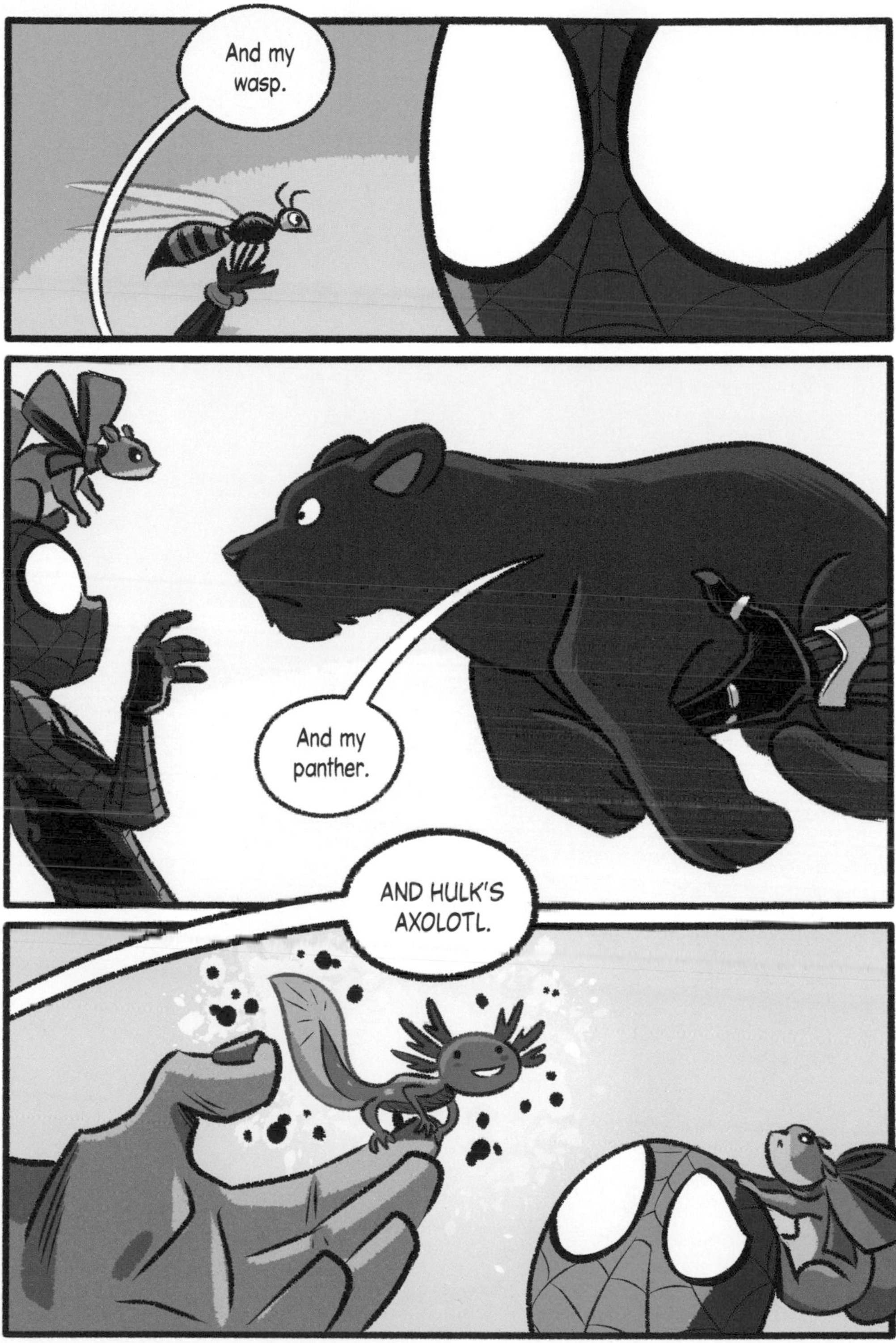
And my wasp.
And my panther.
AND HULK'S AXOLOTL.

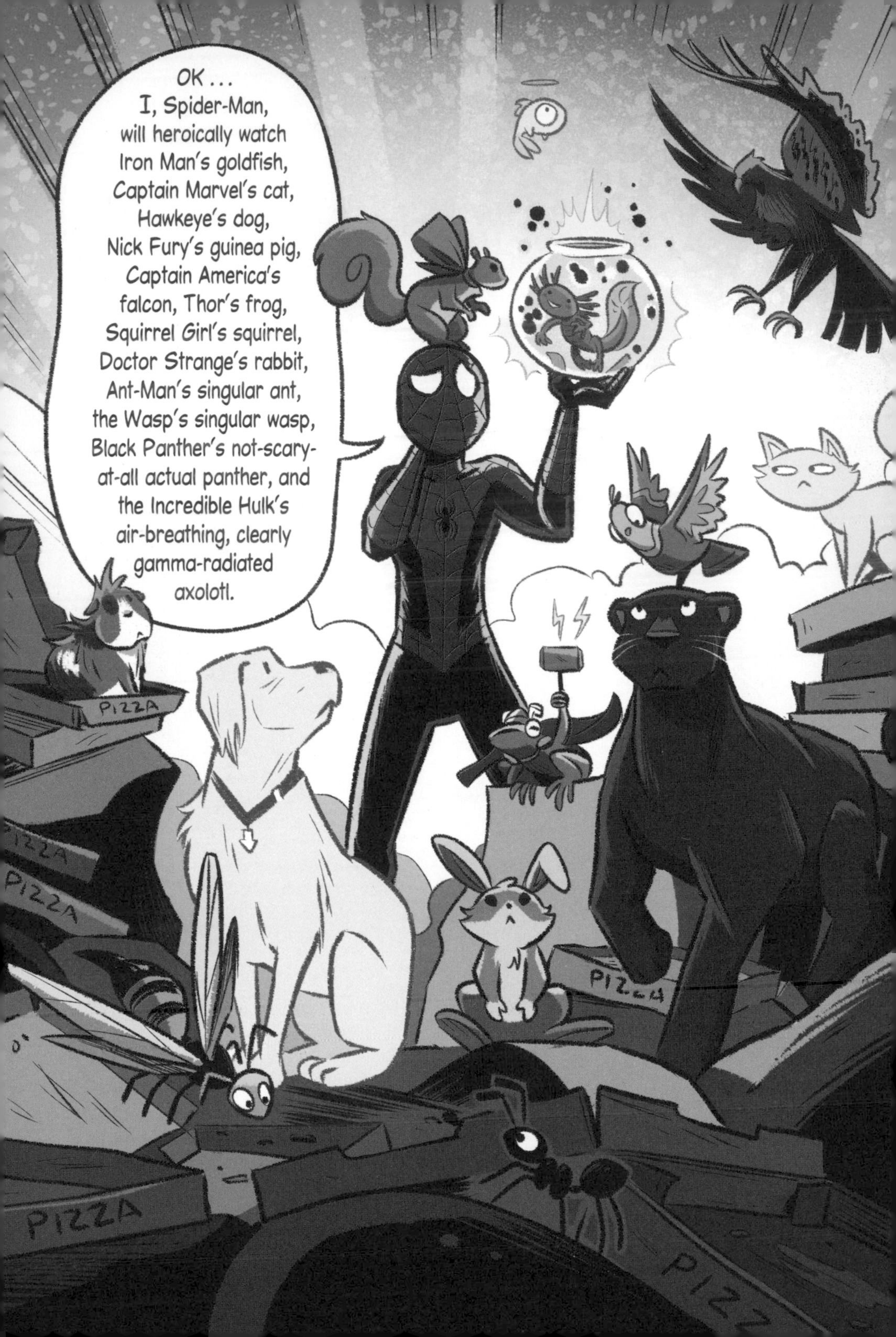
OK . . .
I, Spider-Man, will heroically watch Iron Man's goldfish, Captain Marvel's cat, Hawkeye's dog, Nick Fury's guinea pig, Captain America's falcon, Thor's frog, Squirrel Girl's squirrel, Doctor Strange's rabbit, Ant-Man's singular ant, the Wasp's singular wasp, Black Panther's not-scary-at-all actual panther, and the Incredible Hulk's air-breathing, clearly gamma-radiated axolotl.
PIZZA
PIZZA
PIZZA
PIZZA
PIZZA

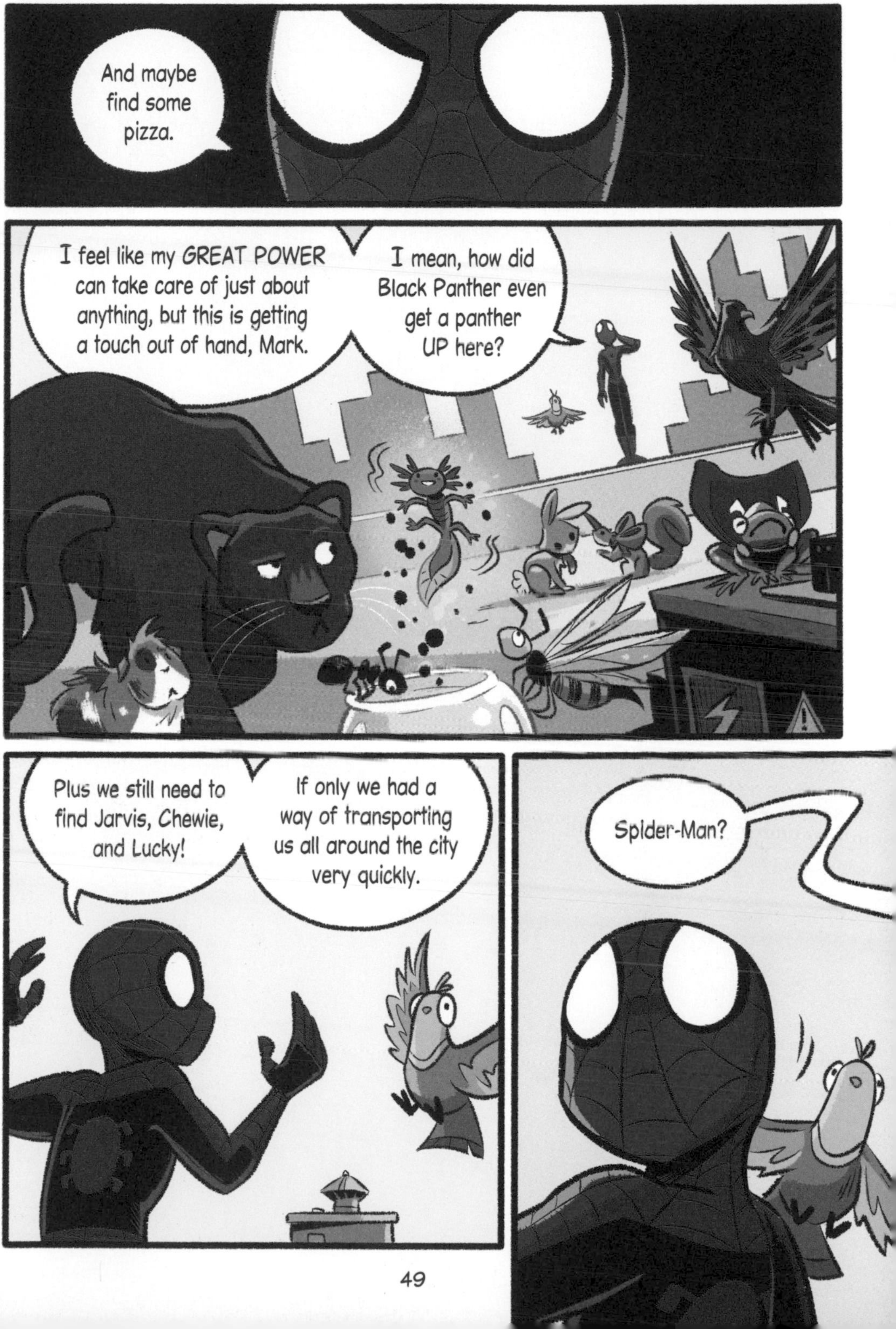
And maybe find some pizza.
I feel like my GREAT POWER can take care of just about anything, but this is getting a touch out of hand, Mark.
I mean, how did Black Panther even get a panther UP here?
Plus we still need to find Jarvis, Chewie, and Lucky!
If only we had a way of transporting us all around the city very quickly.
Spider-Man?

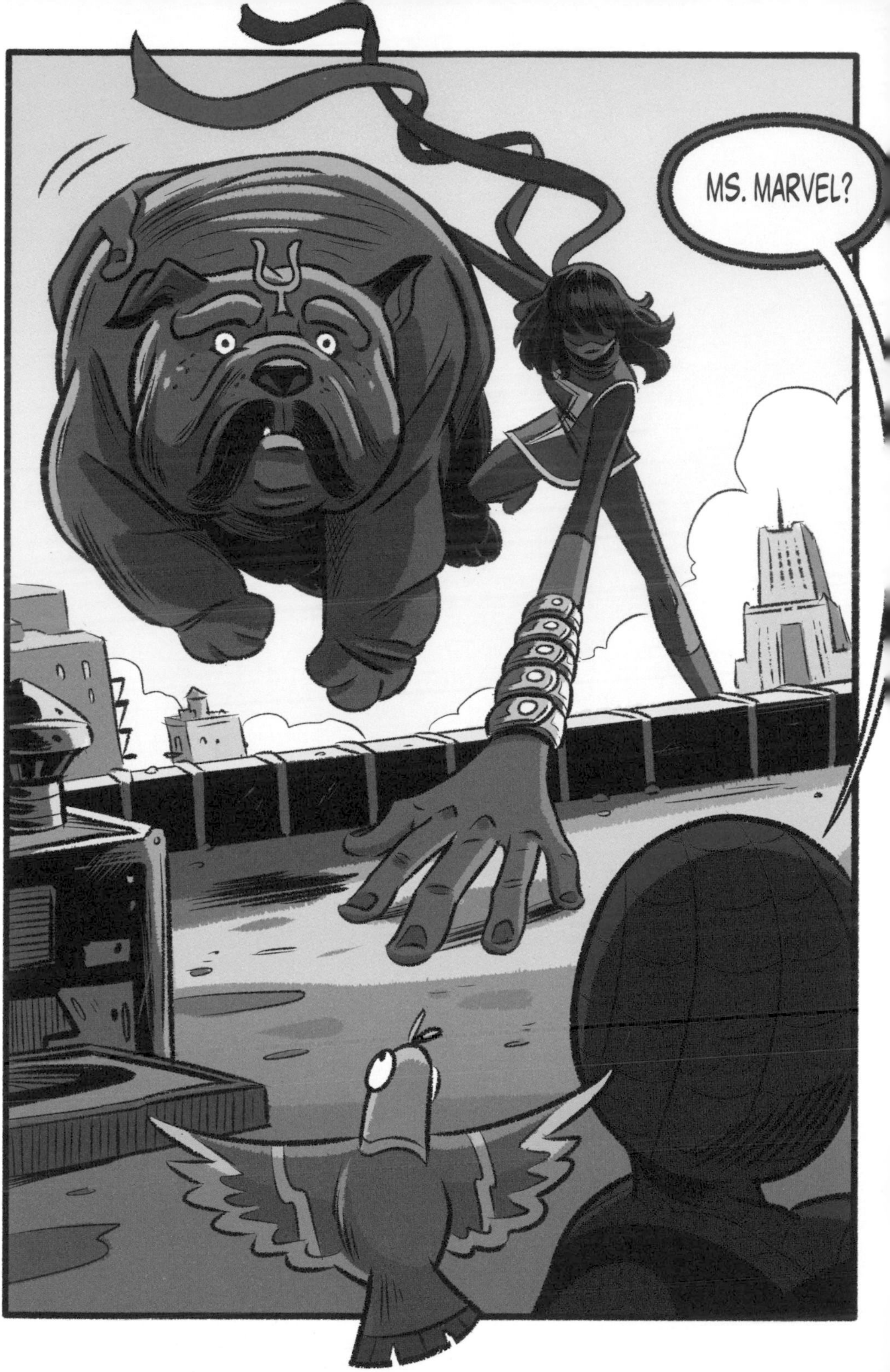
MS. MARVEL?

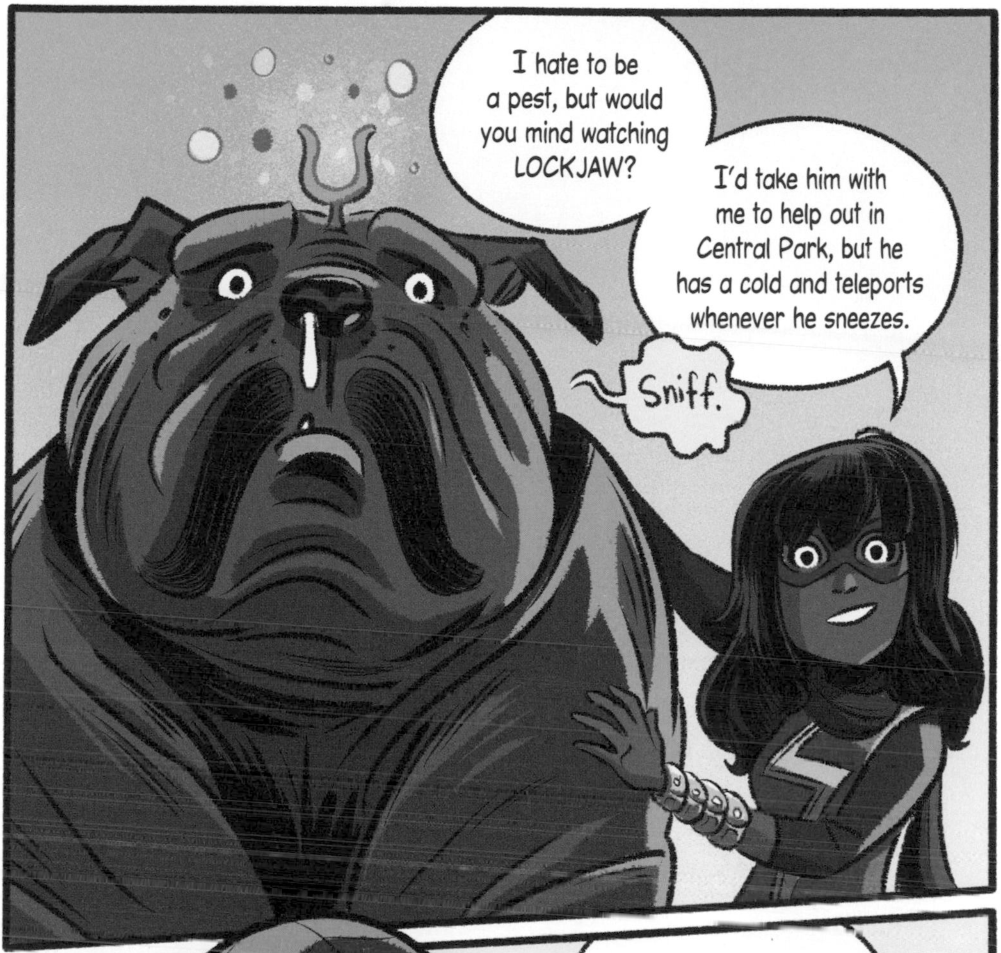
I hate to be a pest, but would you mind watching LOCKJAW?
I'd take him with me to help out in Central Park, but he has a cold and teleports whenever he sneezes.
Sniff.

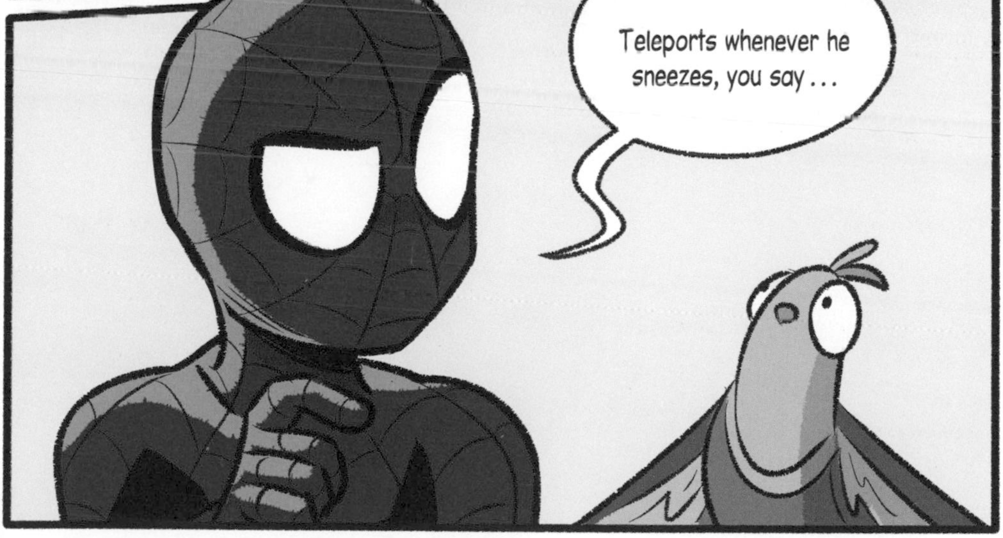
Teleports whenever he sneezes, you say . . .

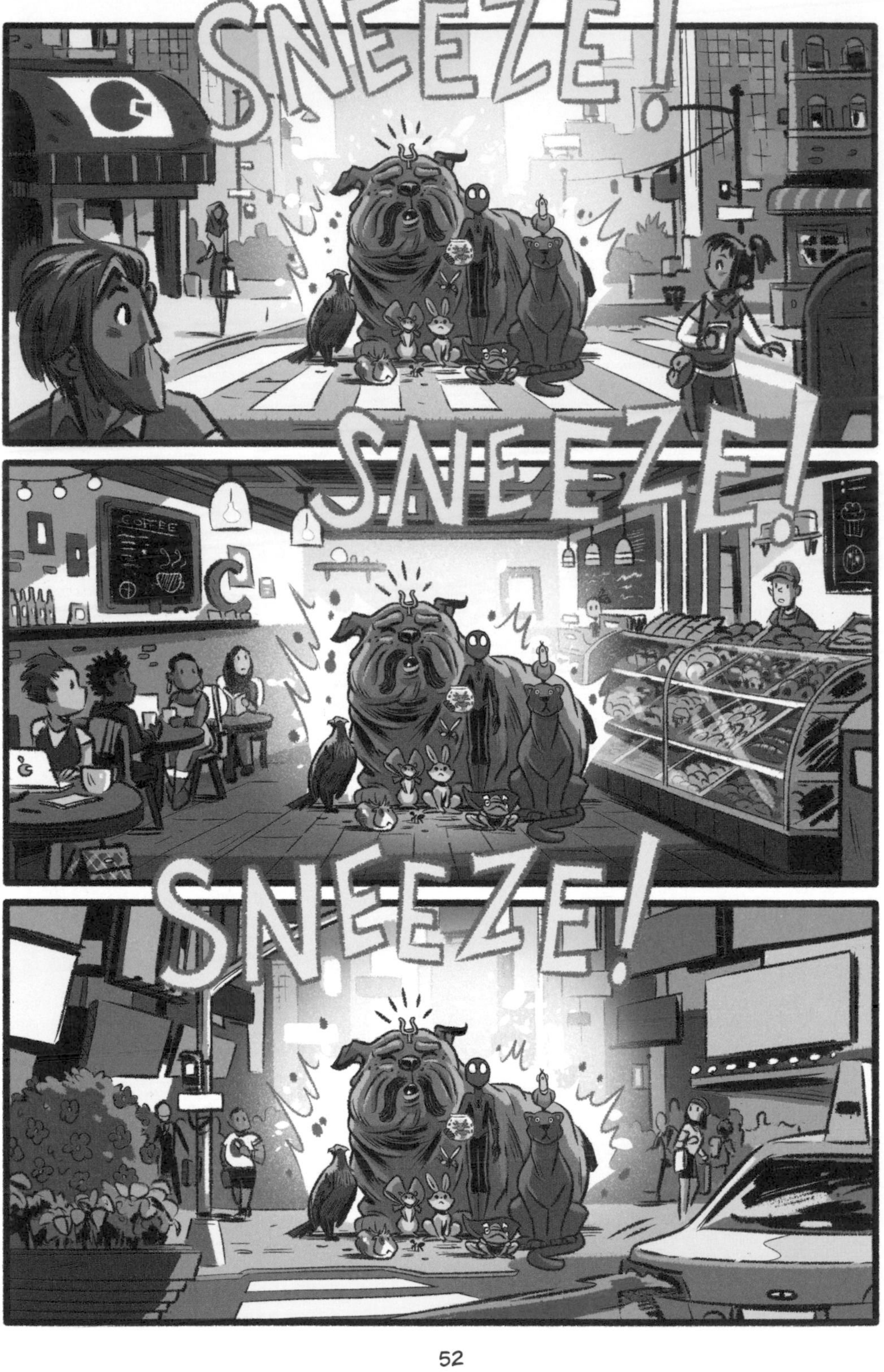
SNEEZE!
SNEEZE!
COFFEE
SNEEZE!

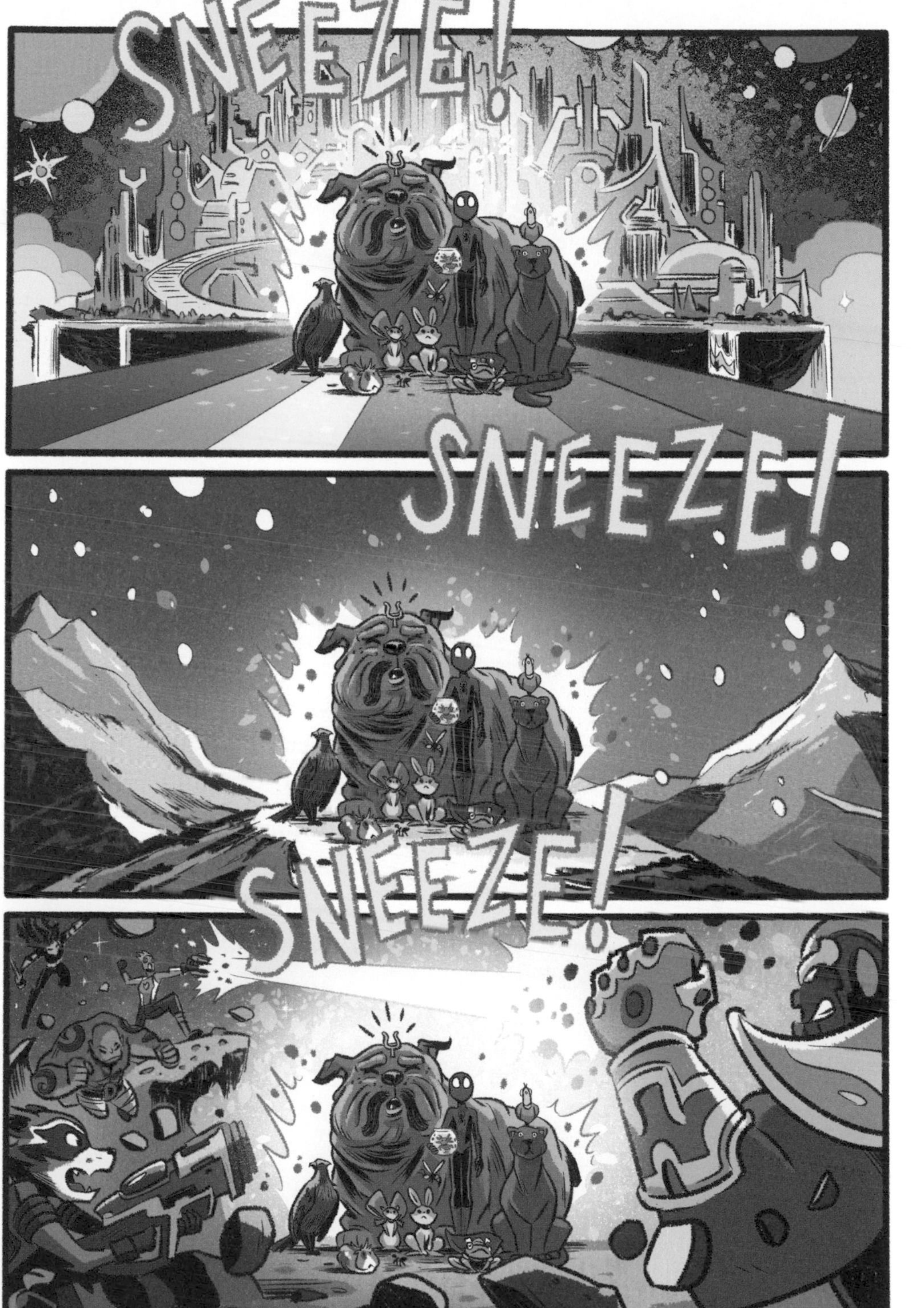
SNEEZE!
SNEEZE!
SNEEZE!

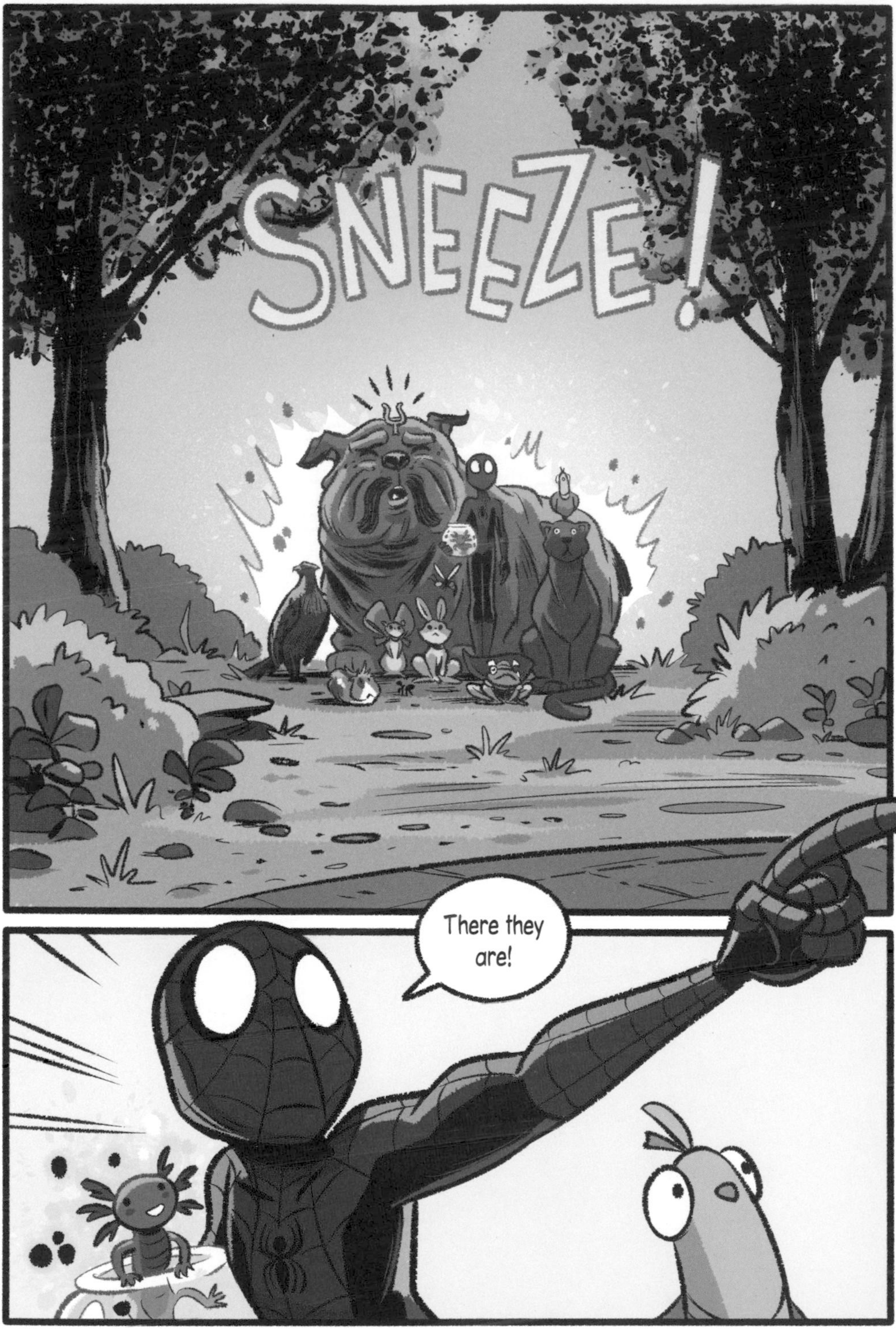
SNEEZE!
There they are!

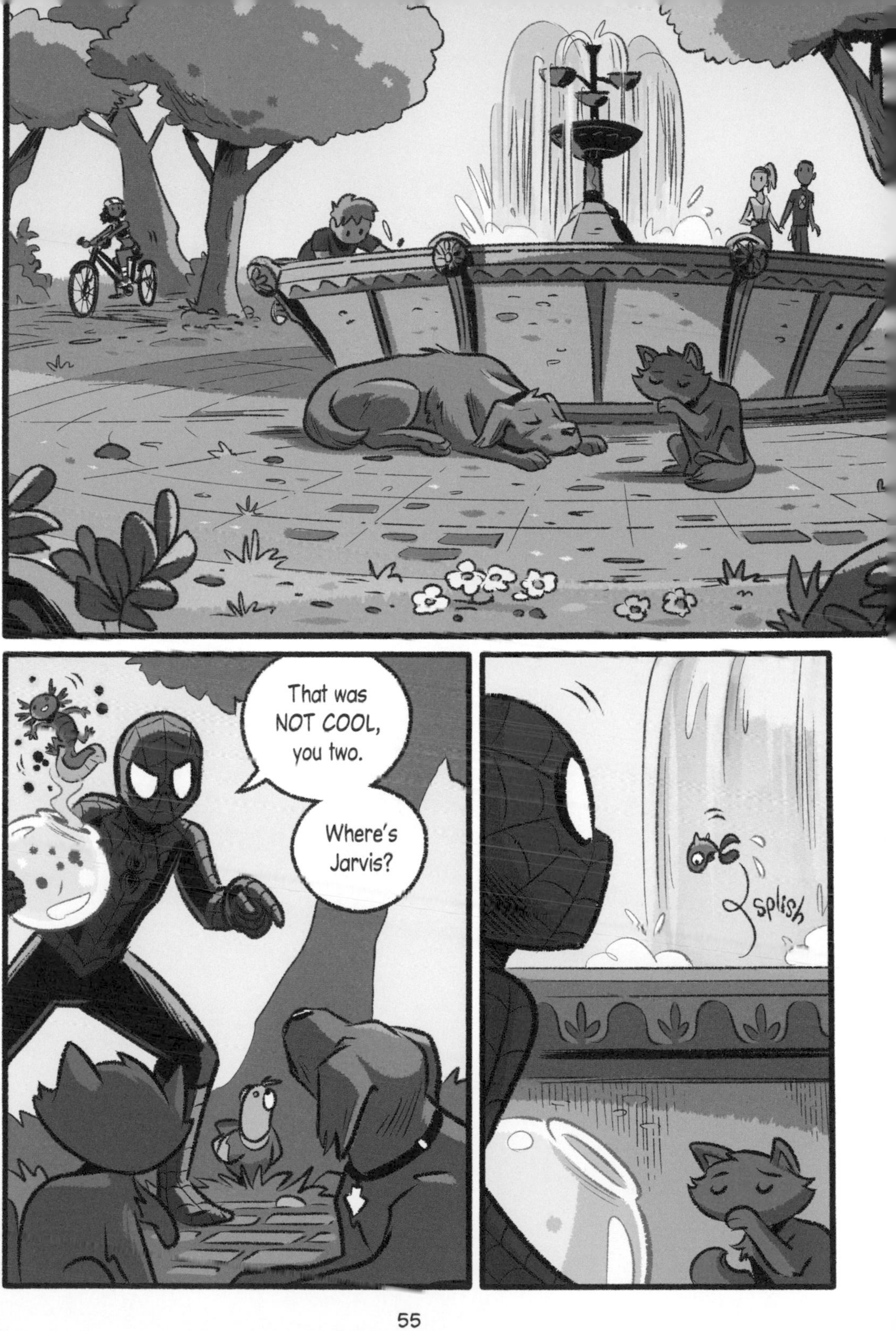
That was NOT COOL, you two.
Where's Jarvis?
splish

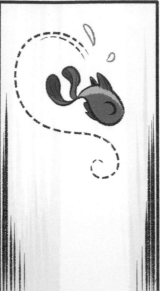

Gotcha!

SPISH

Awesome flip, Jarvis!

Heeeeey . . .

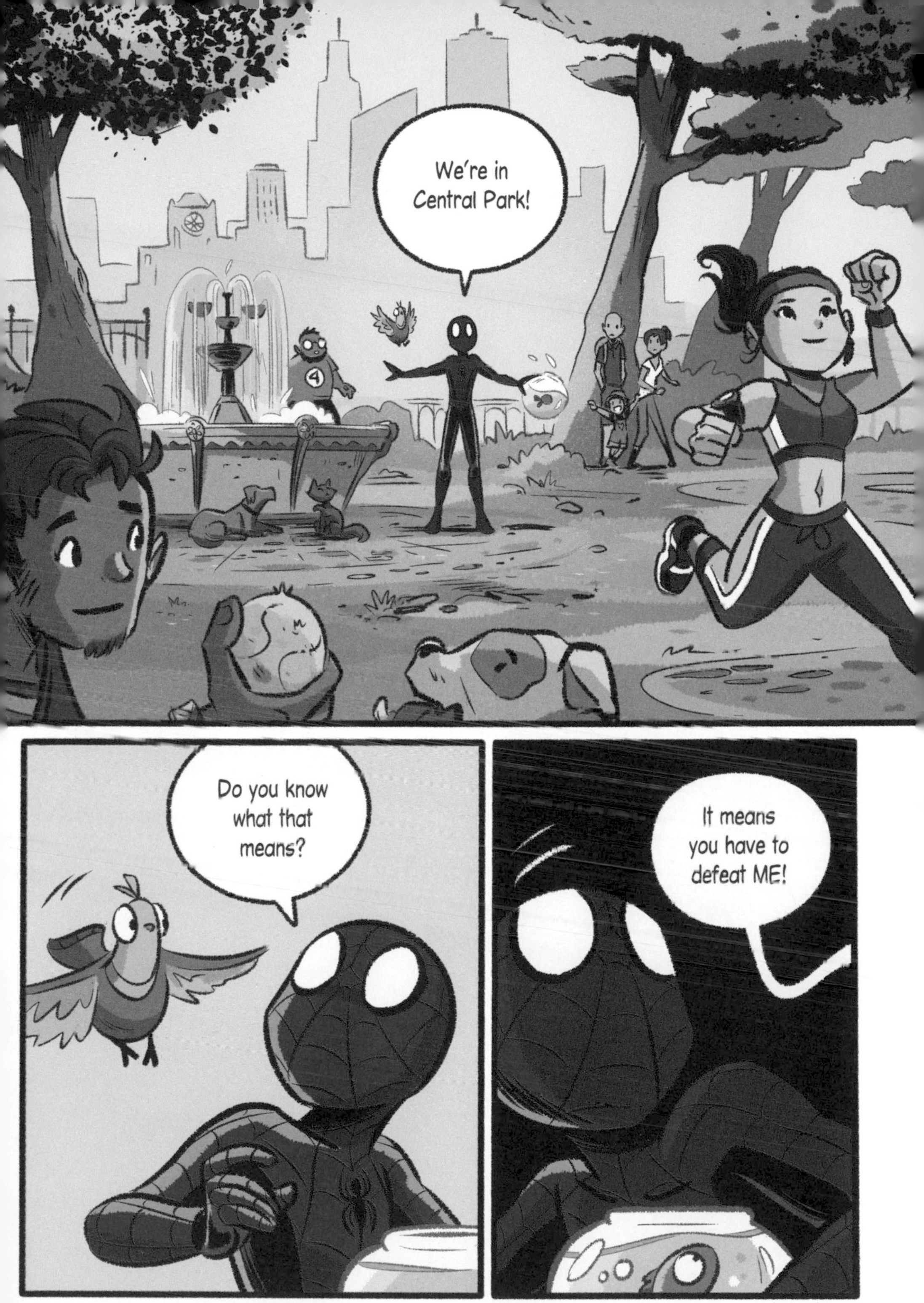
We're in Central Park!
Do you know what that means?
It means you have to defeat ME!

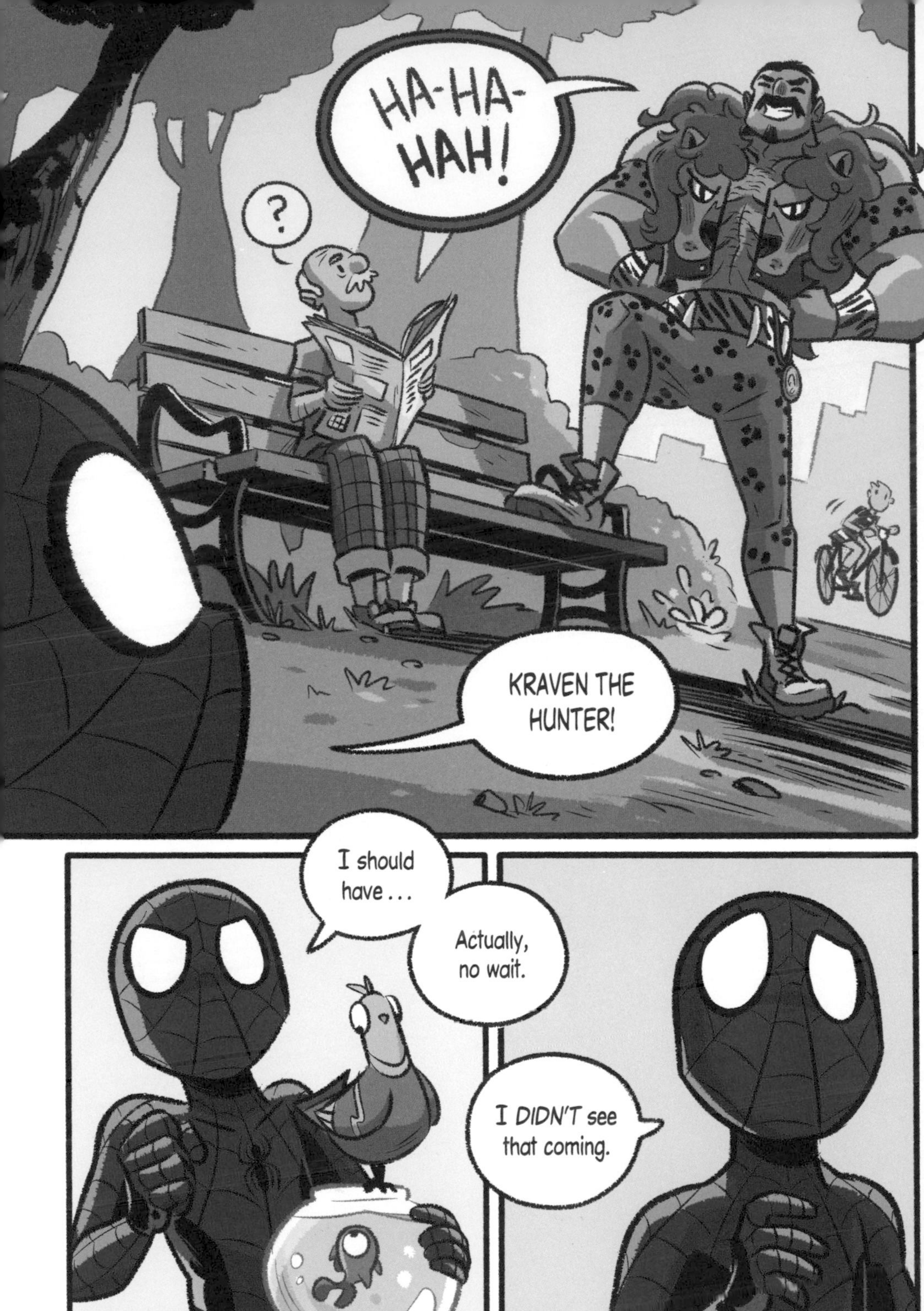
HA-HA-HAH!
?
KRAVEN THE HUNTER!
I should have . . .
Actually, no wait.
I DIDN'T see that coming.

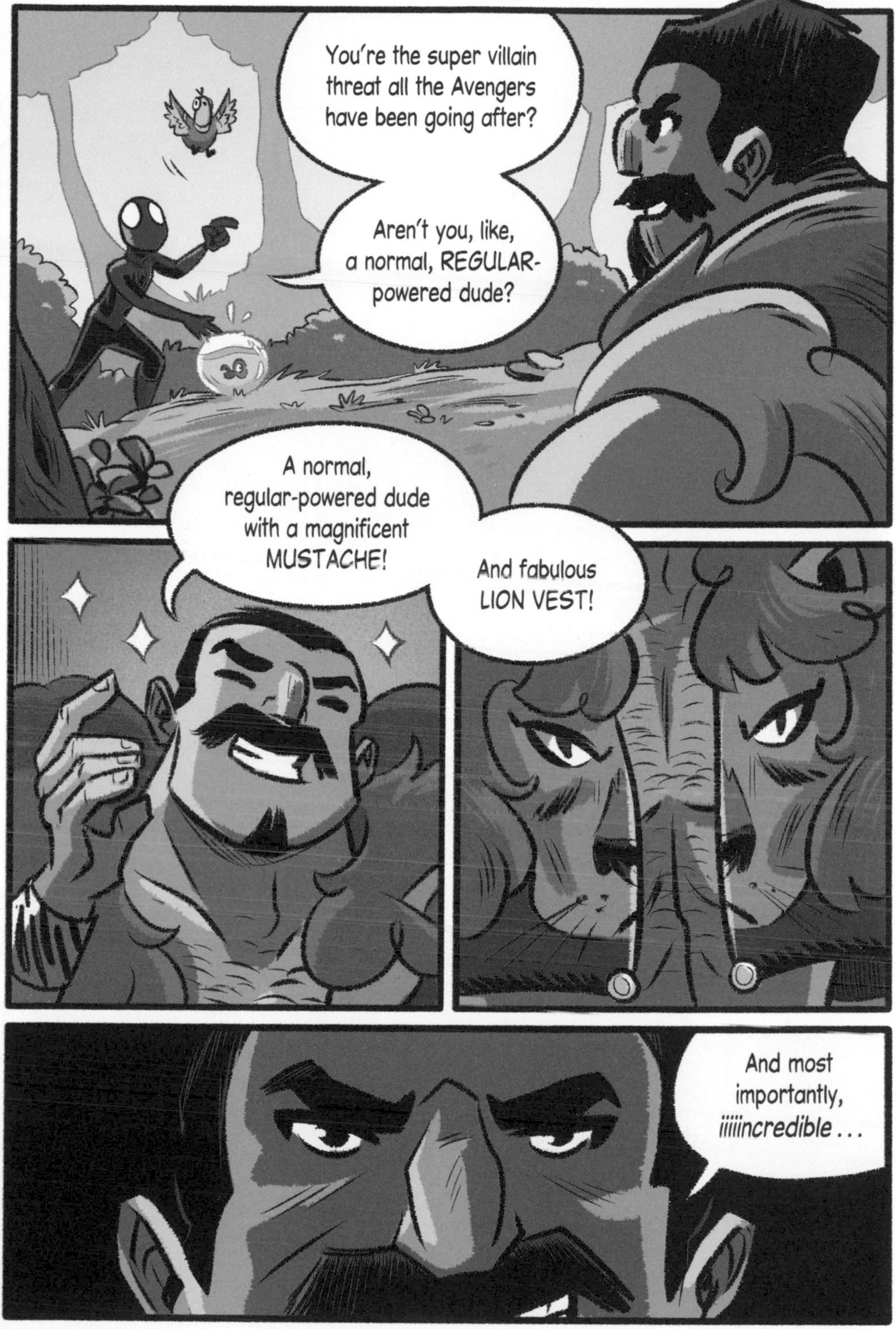
You're the super villain threat all the Avengers have been going after?
Aren't you, like, a normal, REGULAR-powered dude?
A normal, regular-powered dude with a magnificent MUSTACHE!
And fabulous LION VEST!
And most importantly, iiiiincredible . . .

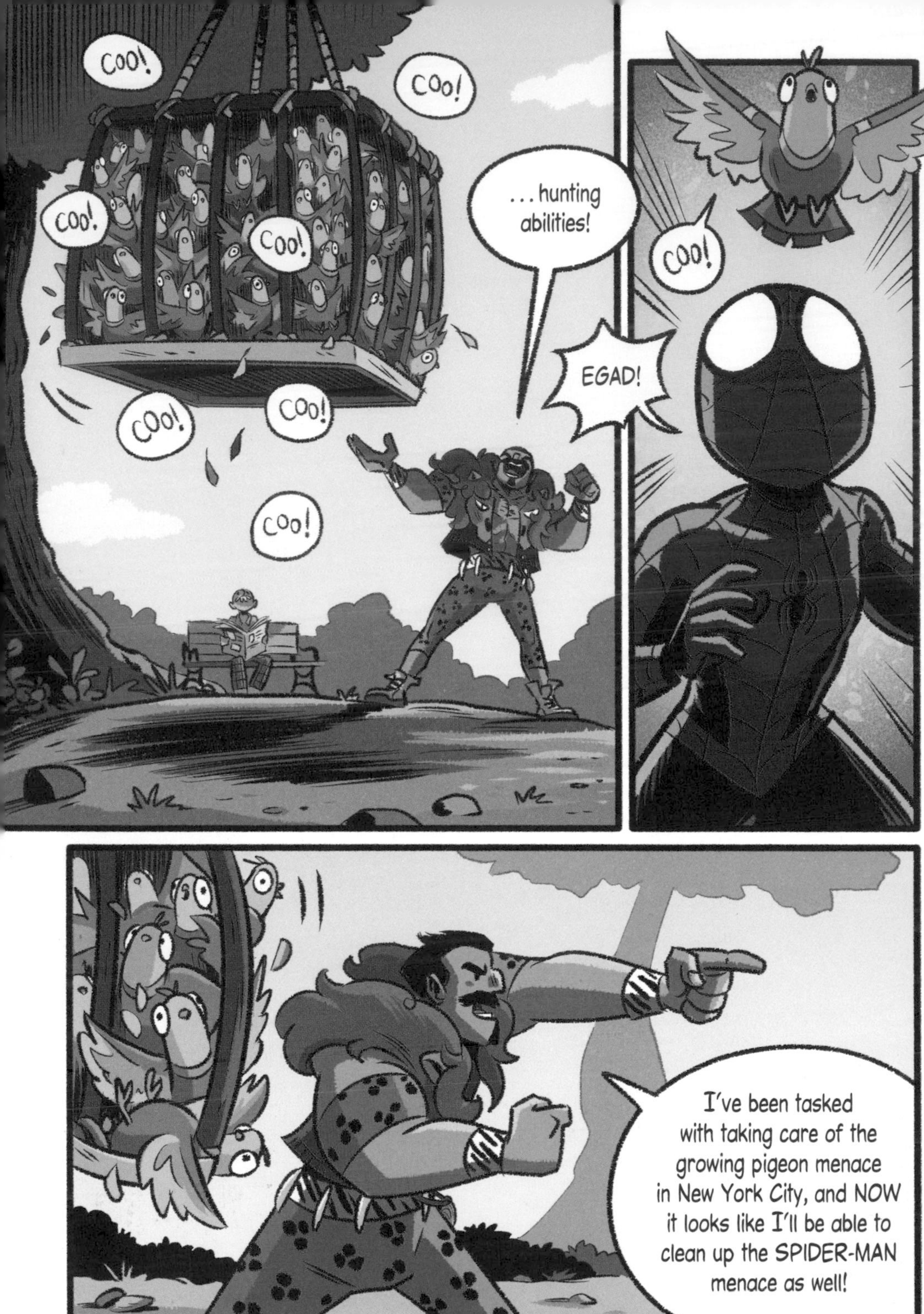
COO!
COO!
COO!
COO!
...hunting abilities!
COO!
COO!
COO!
COO!
EGAD!
I've been tasked with taking care of the growing pigeon menace in New York City, and NOW it looks like I'll be able to clean up the SPIDER-MAN menace as well!

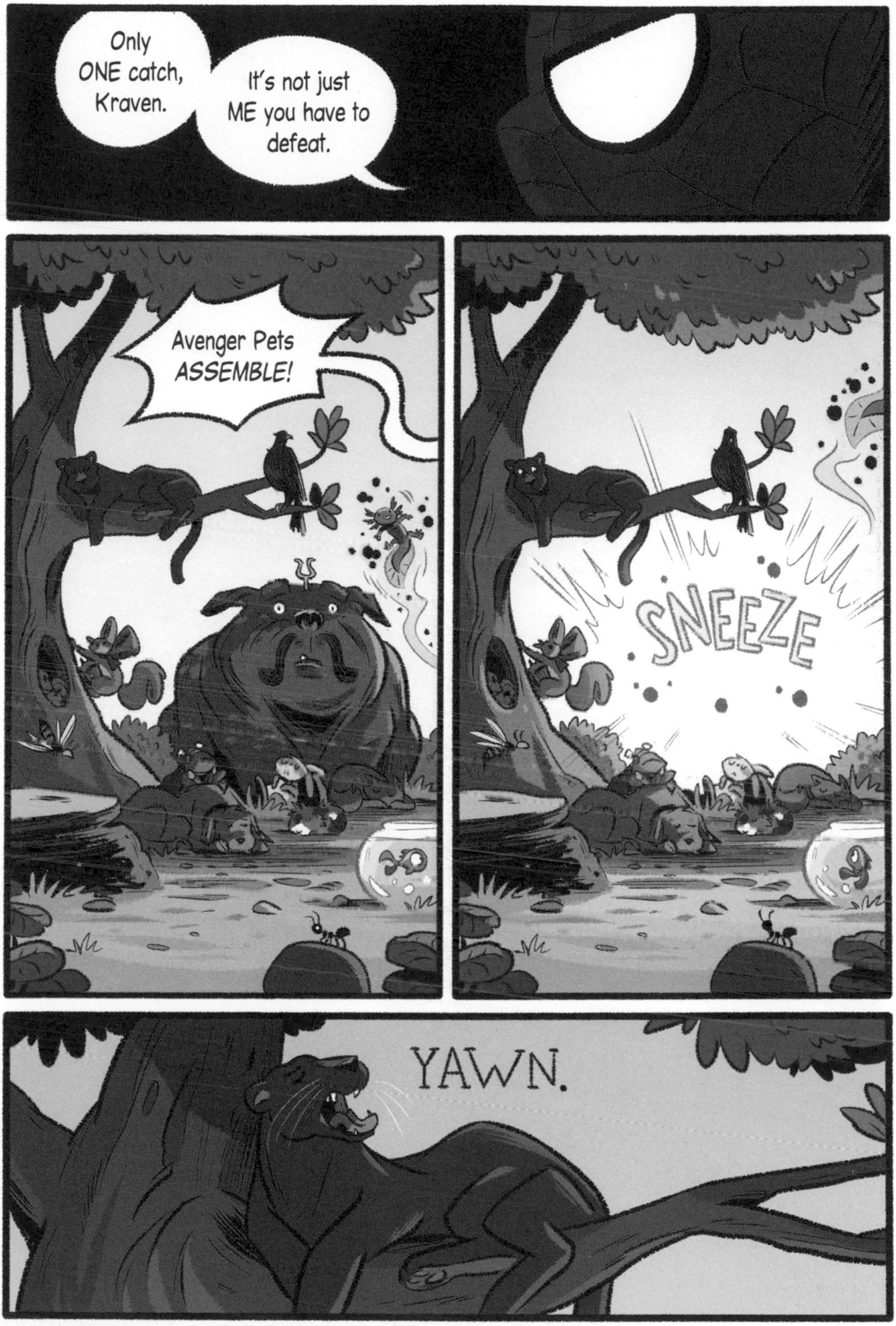
Only ONE catch, Kraven.
It's not just ME you have to defeat.
Avenger Pets ASSEMBLE!
SNEEZE
YAWN.

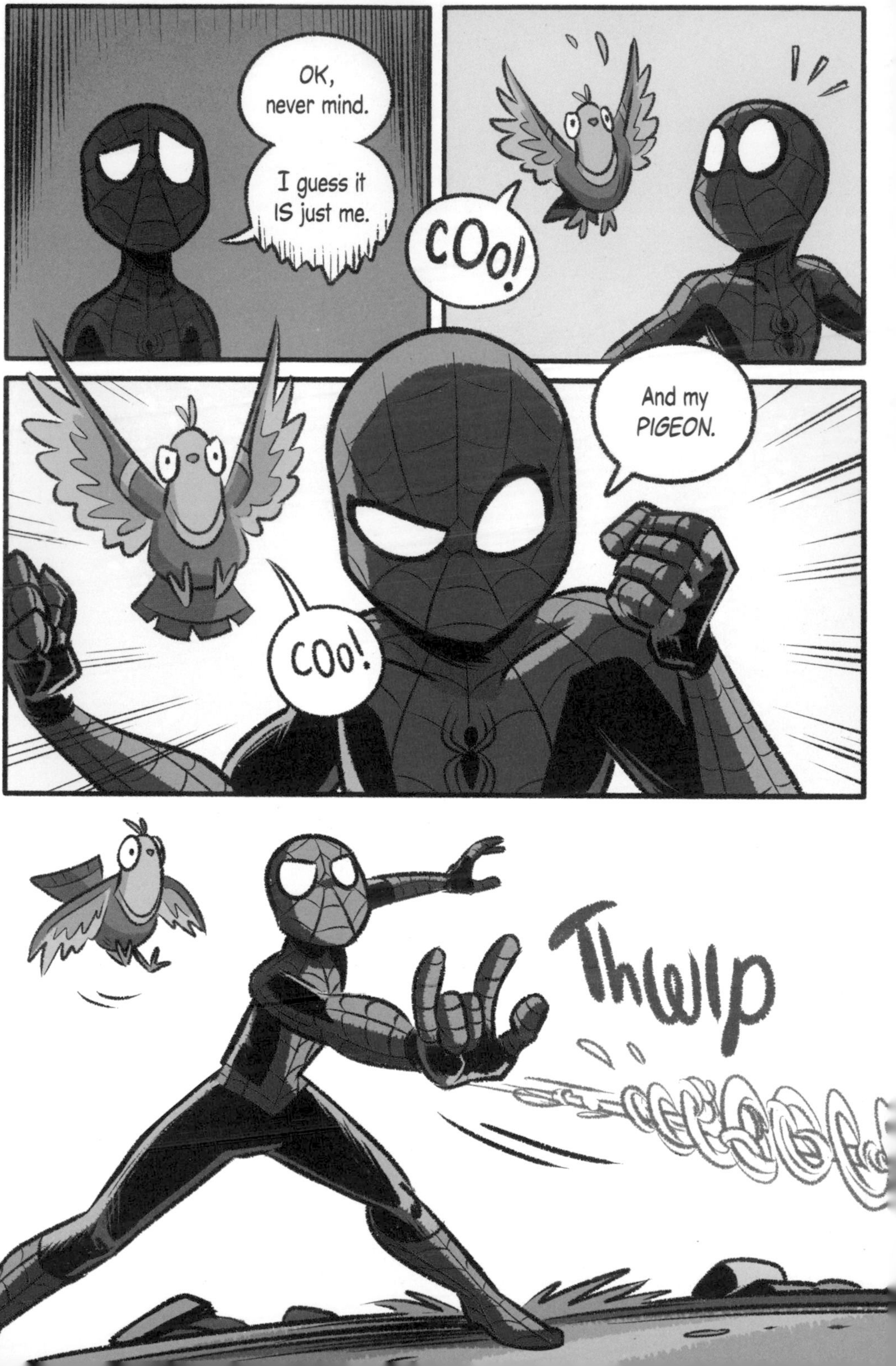
OK, never mind.
I guess it IS just me.
COO!
And my PIGEON.
COO!
THWIP

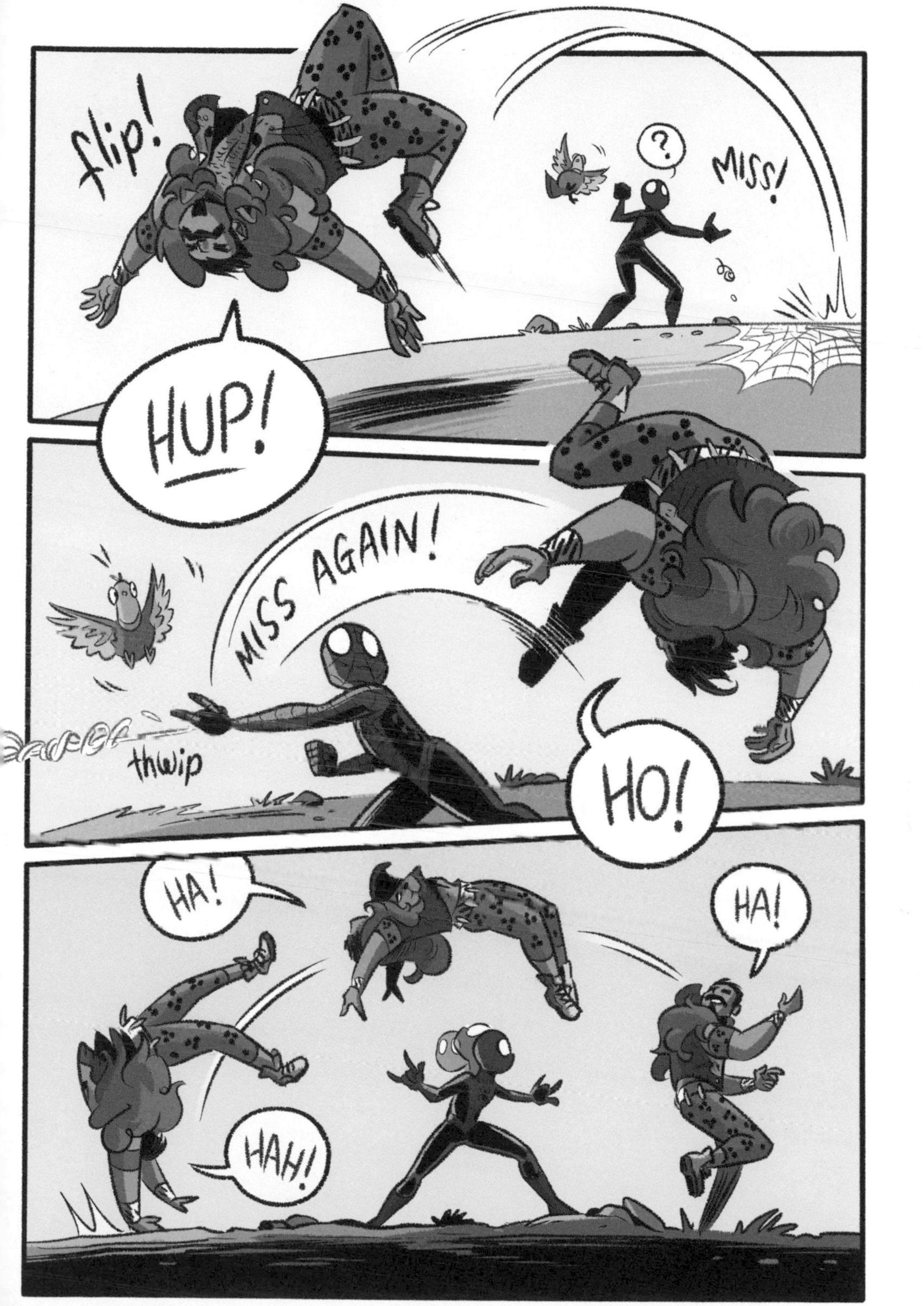
flip!
?
MISS!
HUP!
MISS AGAIN!
thwip
HO!
HA!
HA!
HAH!

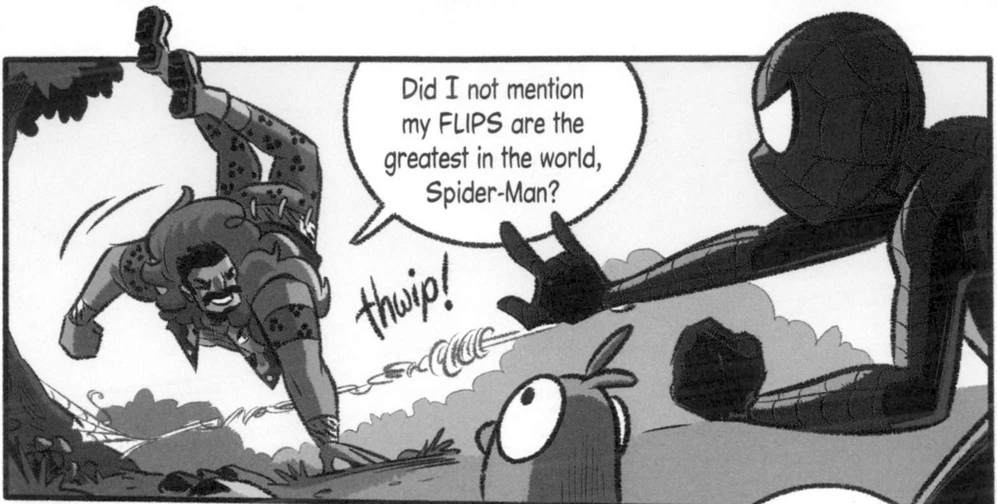
Did I not mention my FLIPS are the greatest in the world, Spider-Man?
thwip!

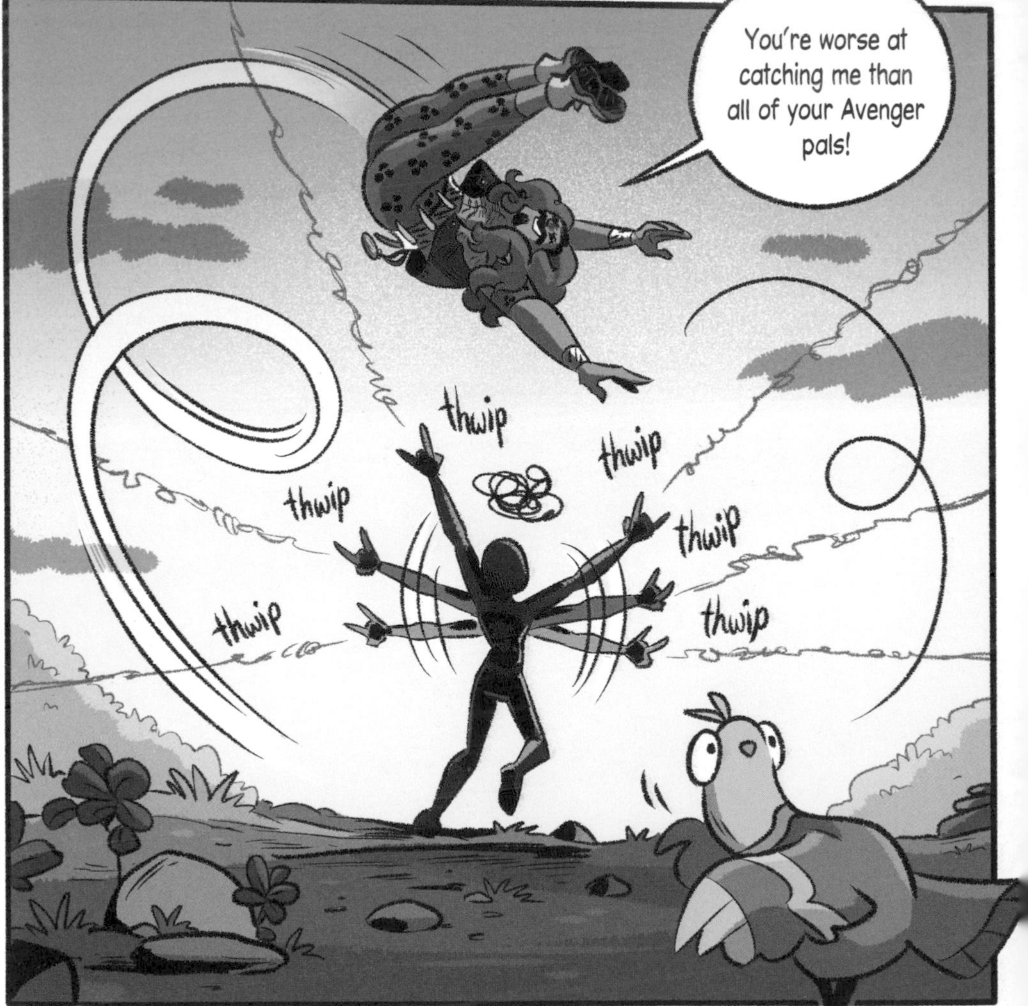
You're worse at catching me than all of your Avenger pals!
thwip
thwip
thwip
thwip
thwip
thwip

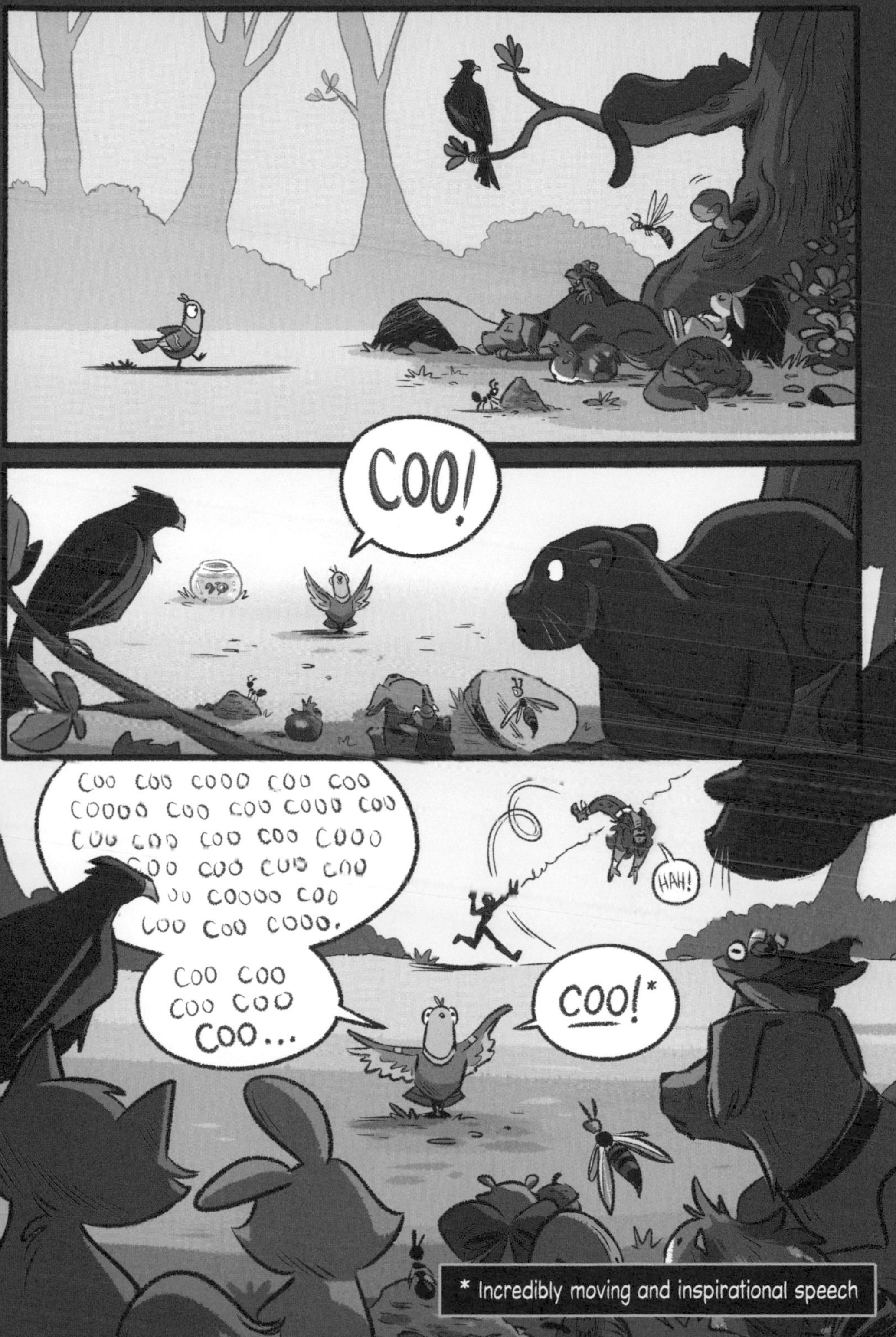
COO!
COO COO COOO COO COO COOOO COO COO COOO COO COO COO COO COO COOO COO COO COO COOOO COO COO COO COOO.
COO COO COO COO COO...
COO!*
HAH!
* Incredibly moving and inspirational speech

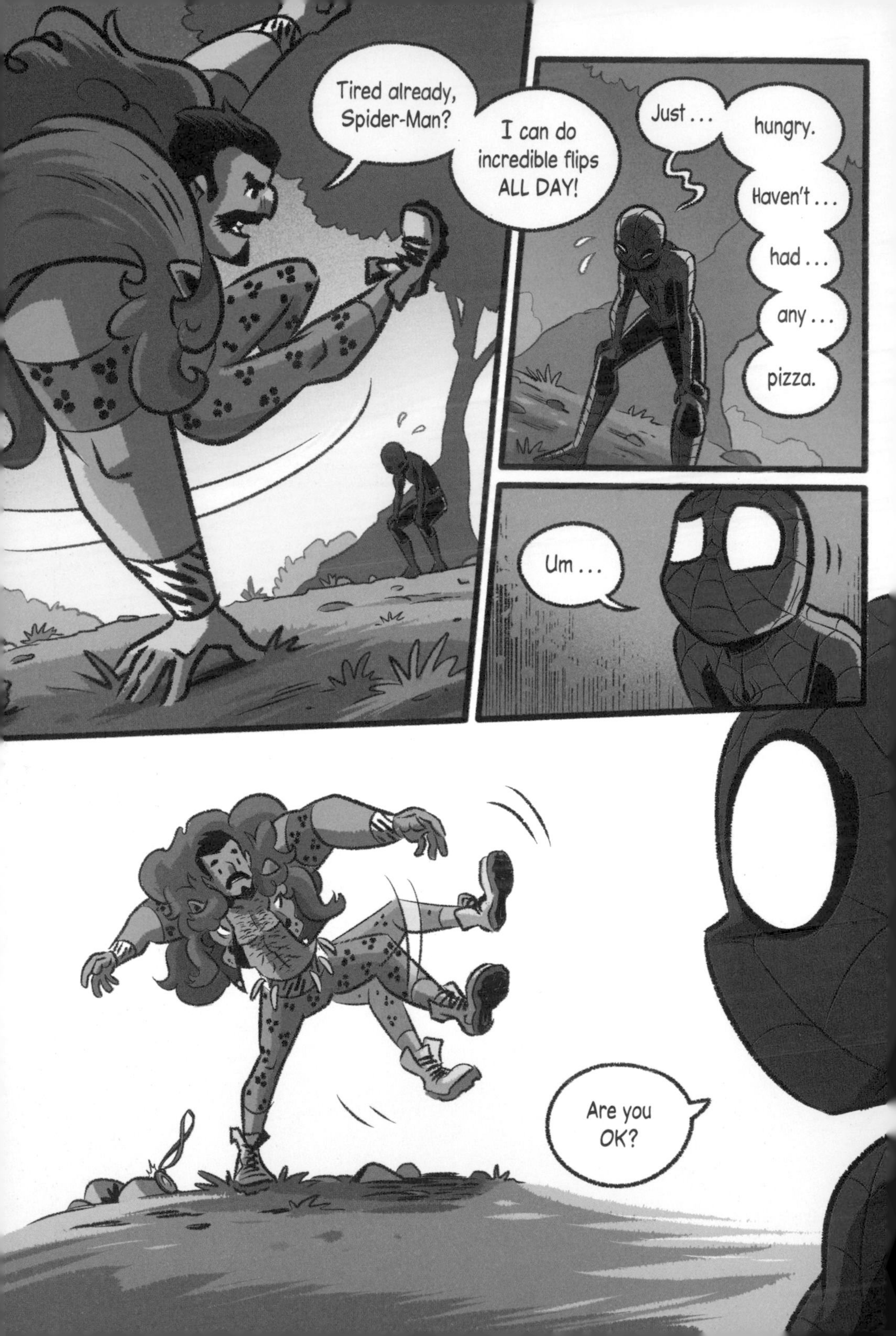
Tired already, Spider-Man?
I can do incredible flips ALL DAY!
Just . . .
hungry.
Haven't . . .
had . . .
any . . .
pizza.
Um . . .
Are you OK?

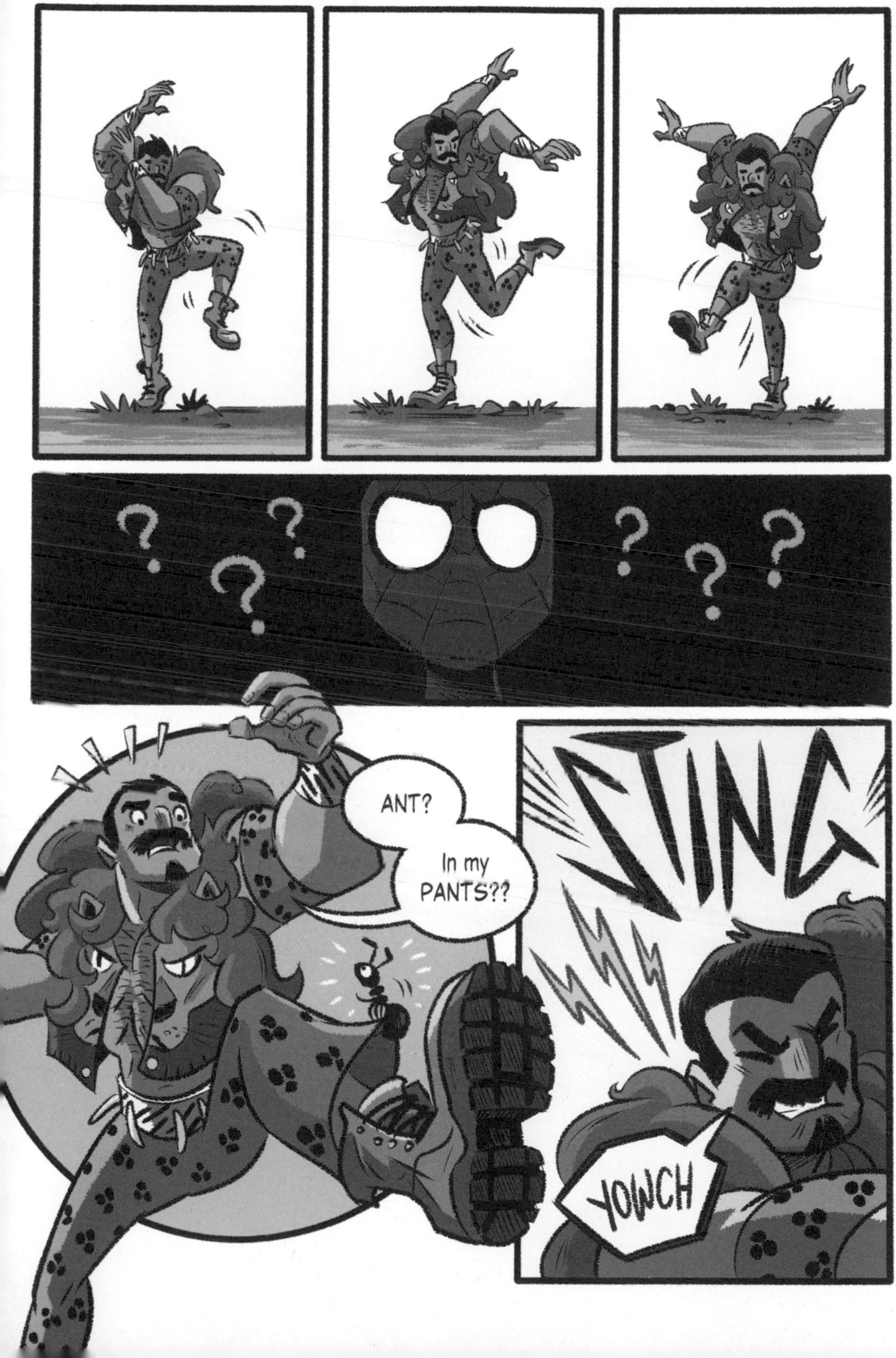

ANT?
In my PANTS??
STING
YOWCH

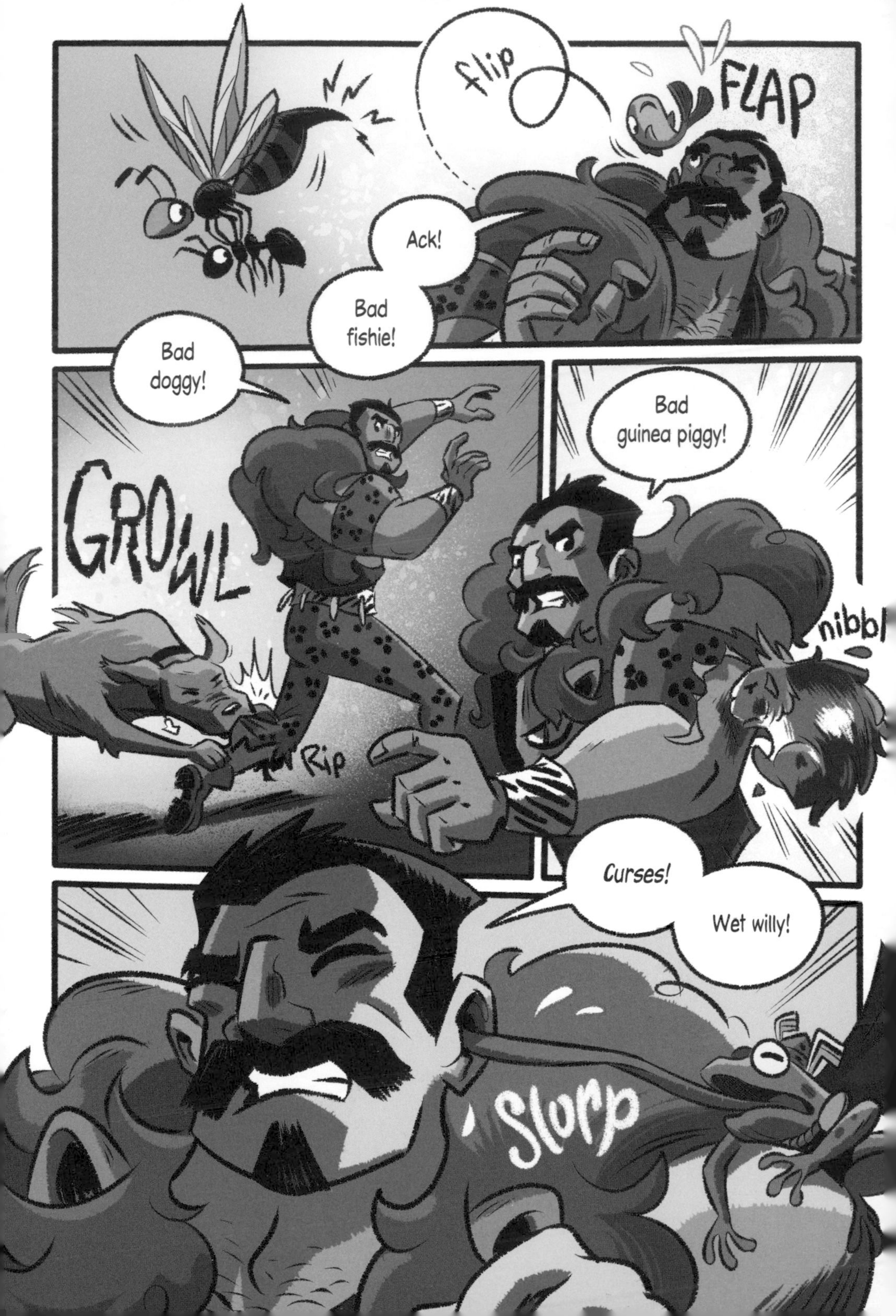

flip
FLAP
Ack!
Bad fishie!
Bad doggy!
GROWL
Rip
Bad guinea piggy!
nibbl
Curses!
Wet willy!
Slorp

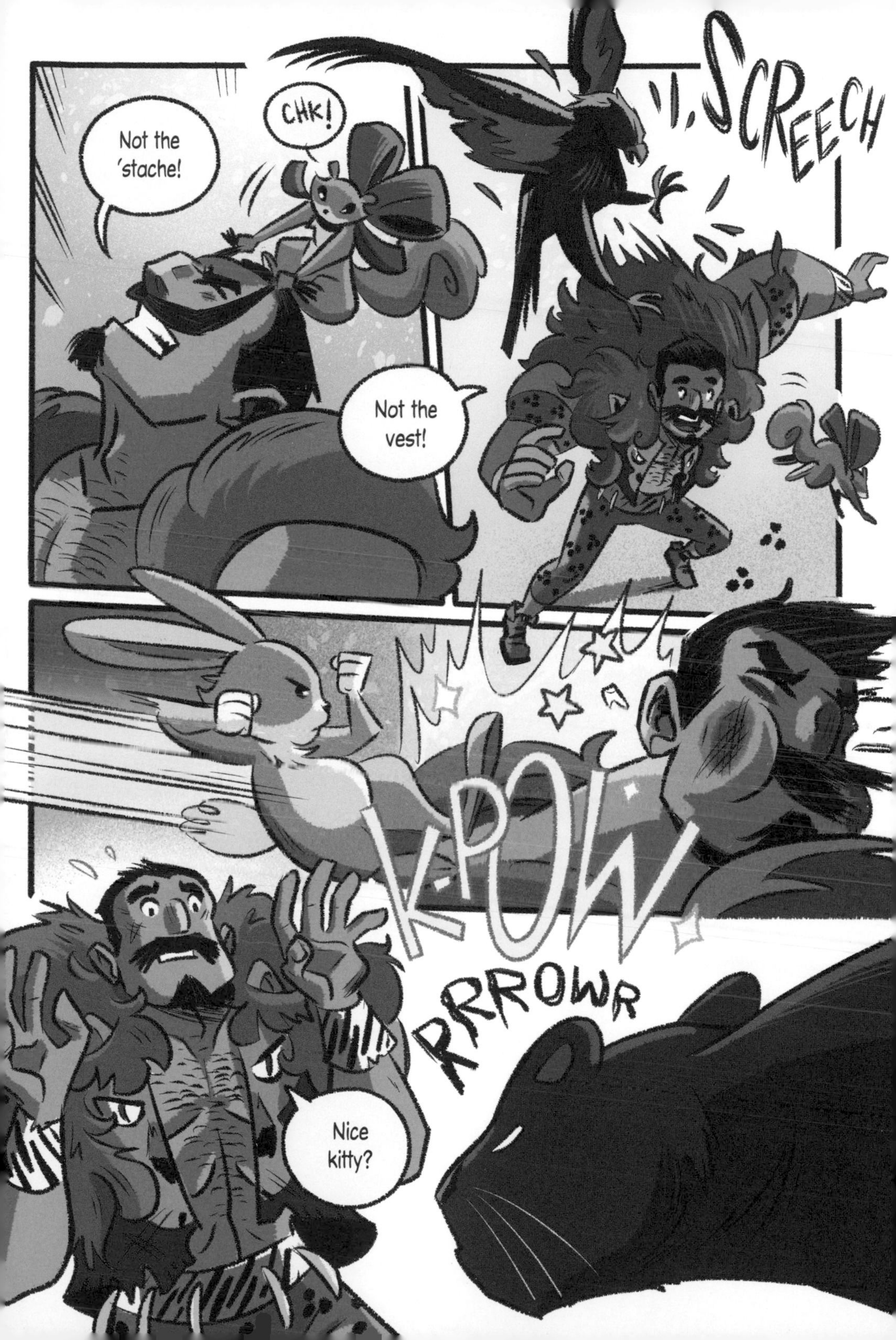
Not the 'stache!
CHK!
SCREECH
Not the vest!
K-POW
RRROWR
Nice kitty?

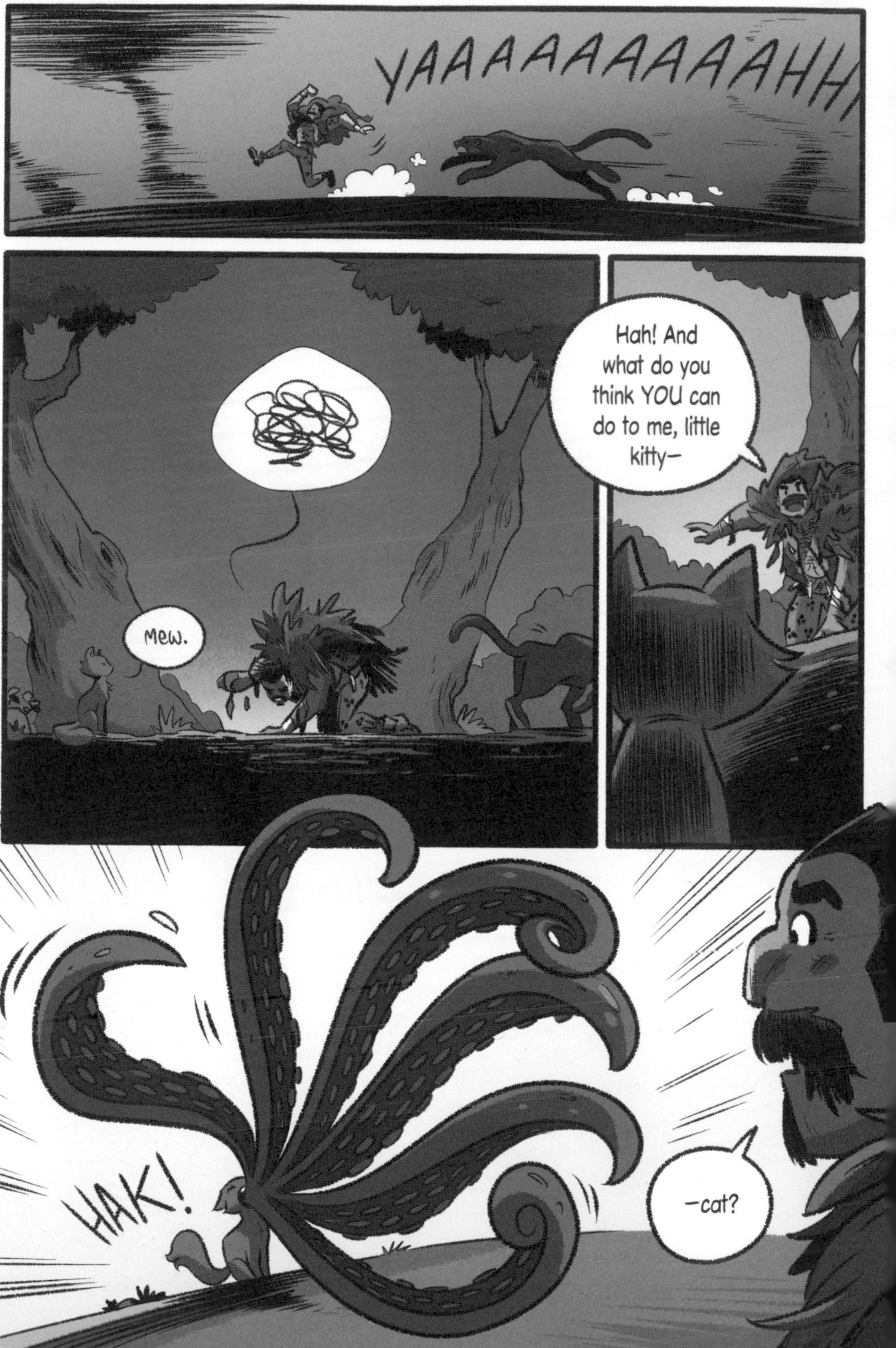
YAAAAAAAAAAHH
Mew.
Hah! And what do you think YOU can do to me, little kitty—
HAK!
—cat?

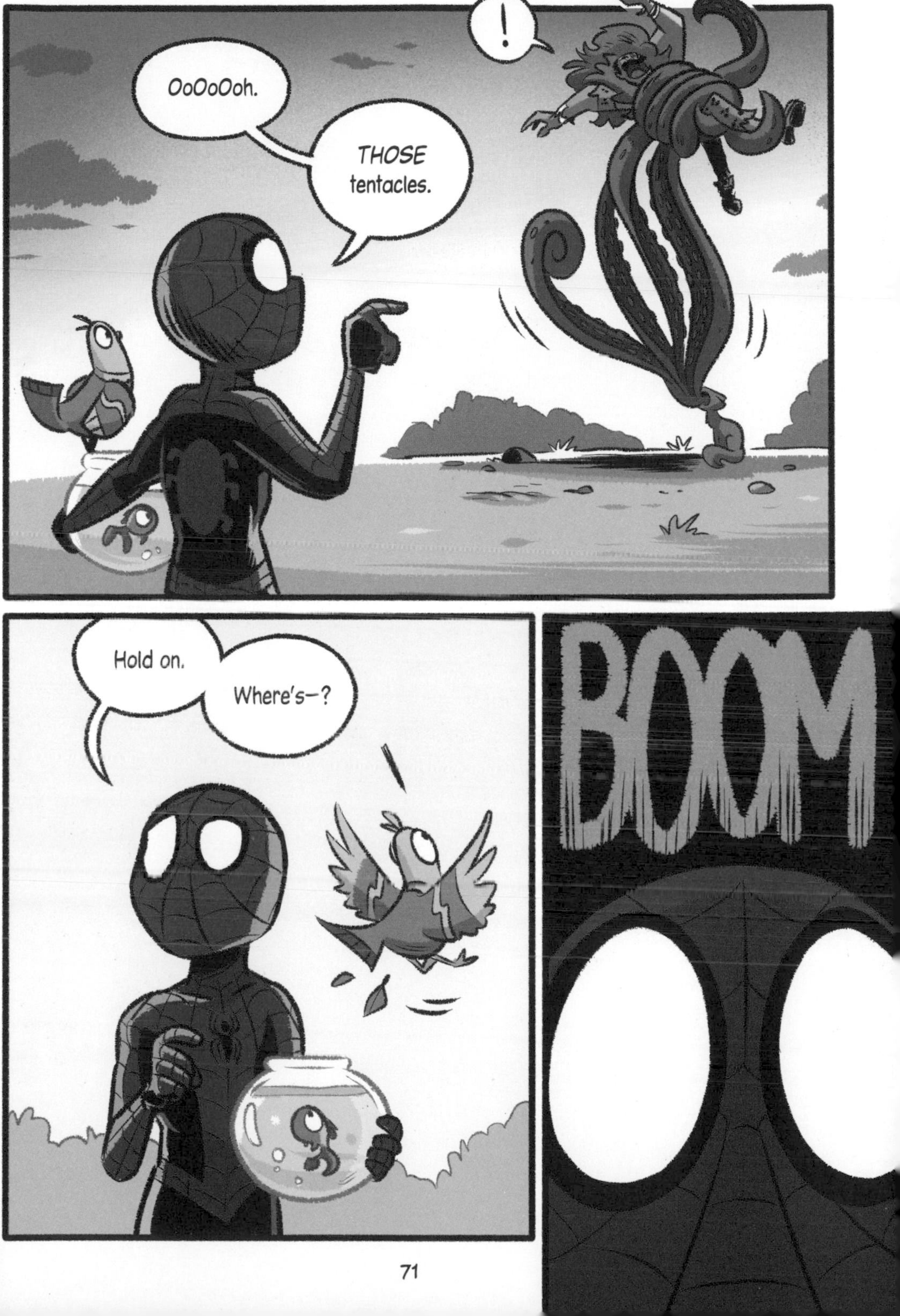
OoOoOoh.
THOSE tentacles.
!
Hold on.
Where's—?
BOOM

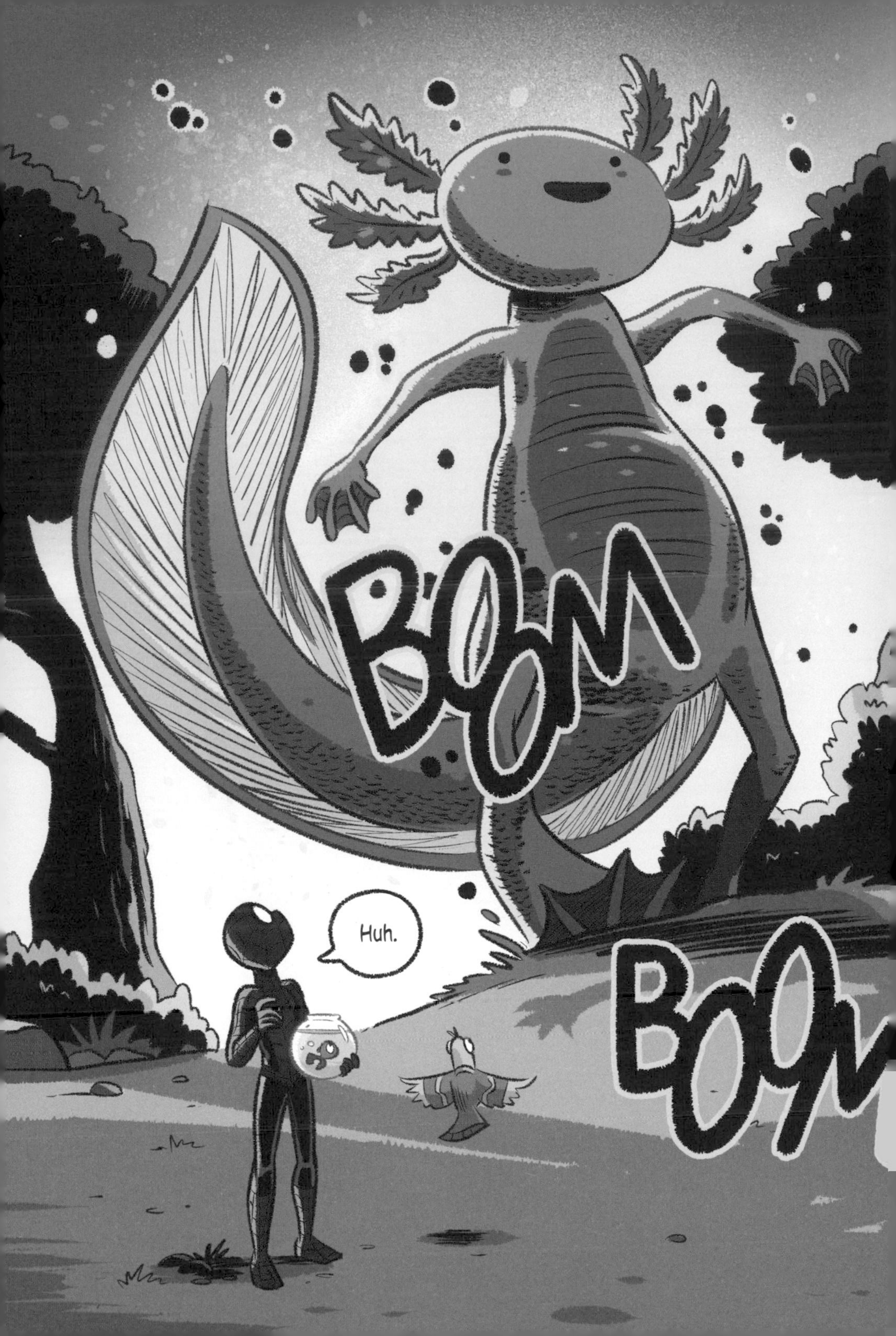
BOOM
Huh.
BOOM

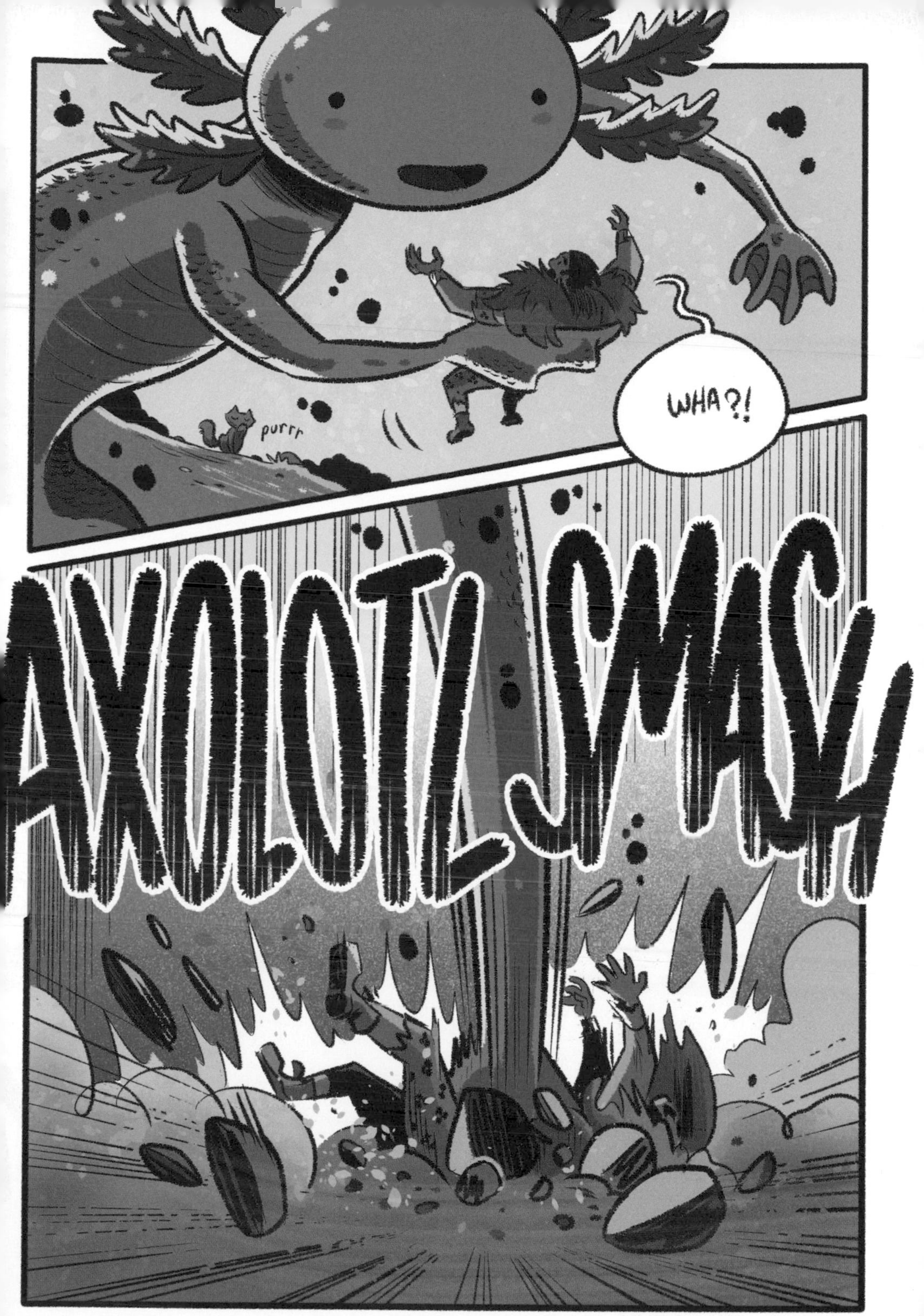
purrr
WHA?!
AXOLOTL SMASH

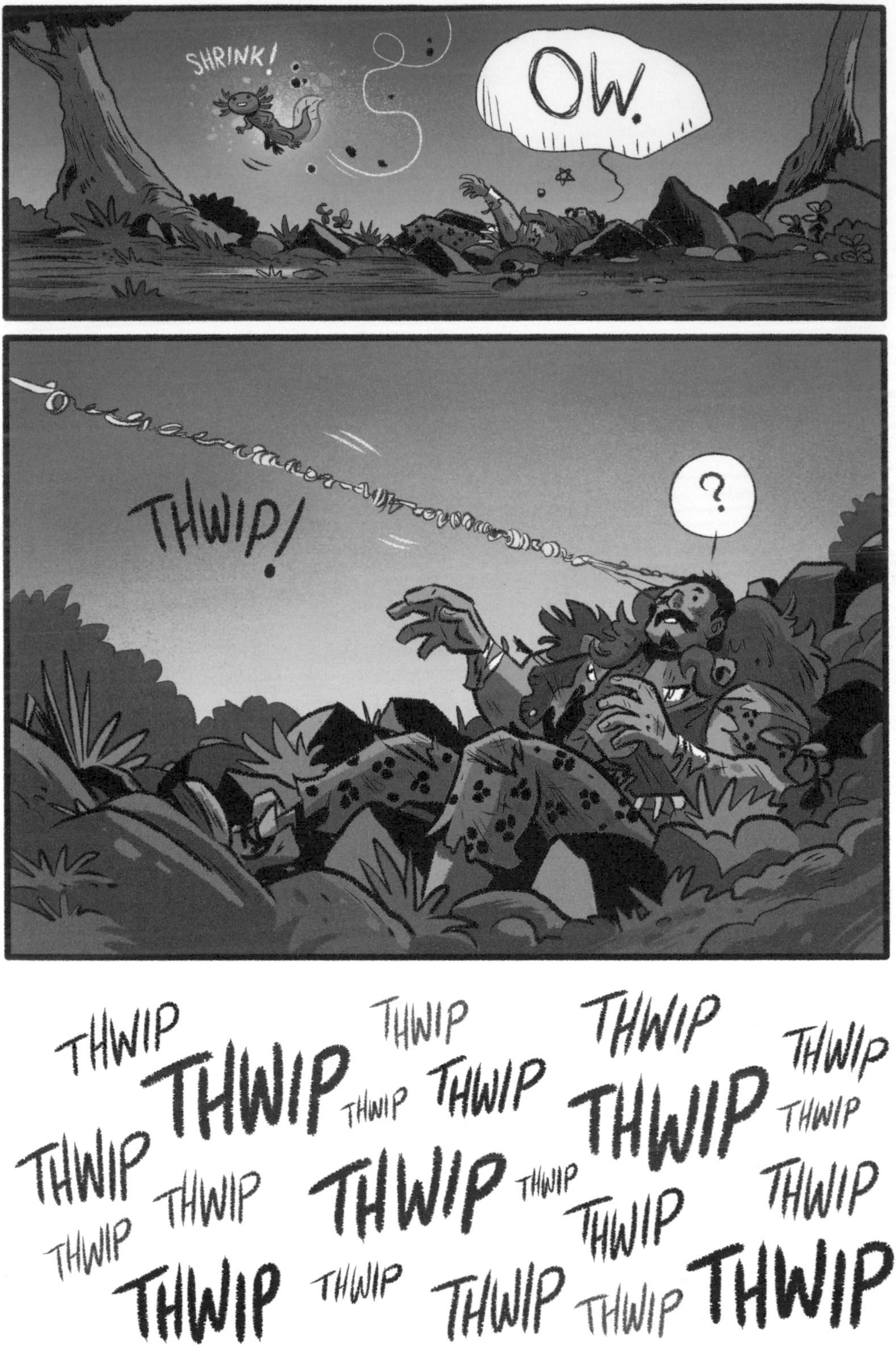
SHRINK!
OW.
THWIP!
?
THWIP
THWIP
THWIP
THWIP
THWIP
THWIP
THWIP
THWIP
THWIP
THWIP
THWIP
THWIP
THWIP
THWIP
THWIP
THWIP
THWIP
THWIP
THWIP
THWIP
THWIP

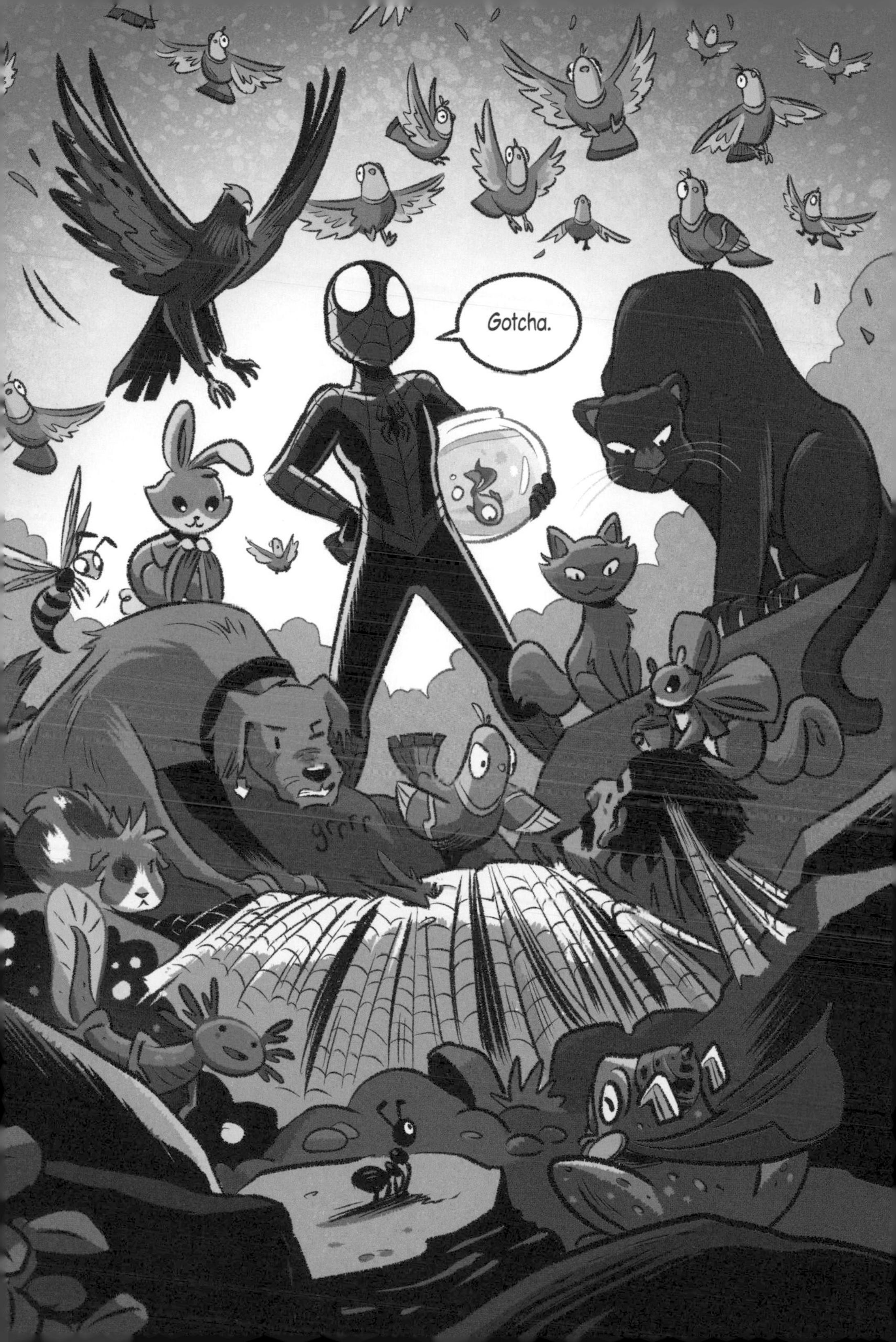
Gotcha.
grrrr

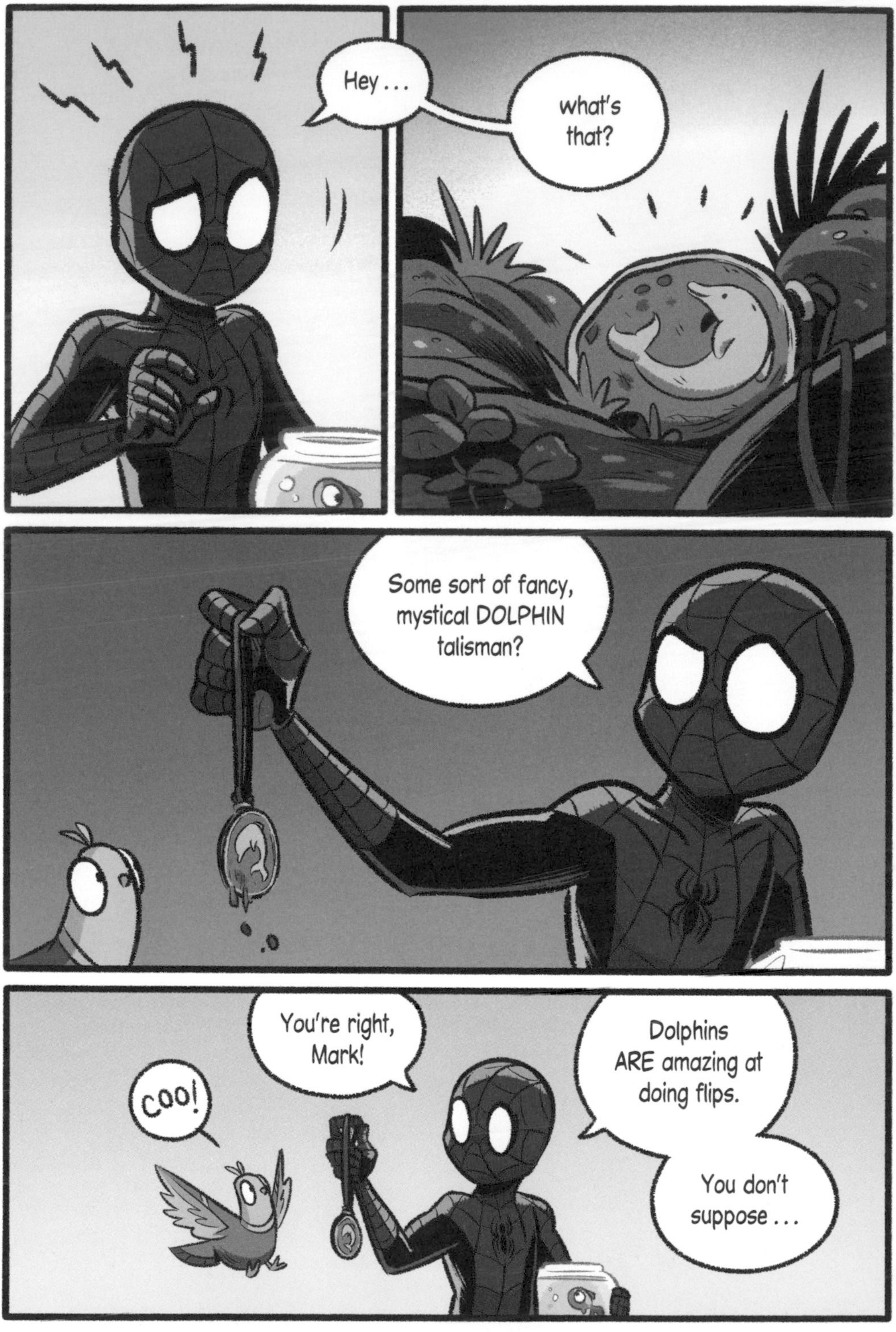

Hey . . .
what's that?
Some sort of fancy, mystical DOLPHIN talisman?
COO!
You're right, Mark!
Dolphins ARE amazing at doing flips.
You don't suppose . . .

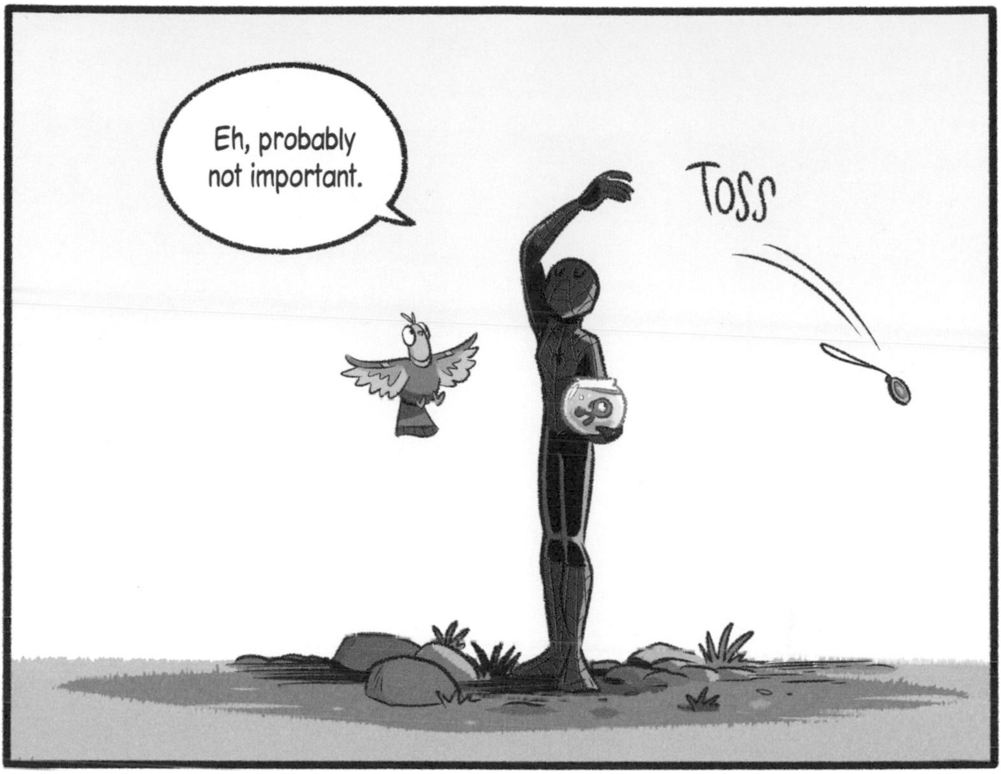
Eh, probably not important.
TOSS

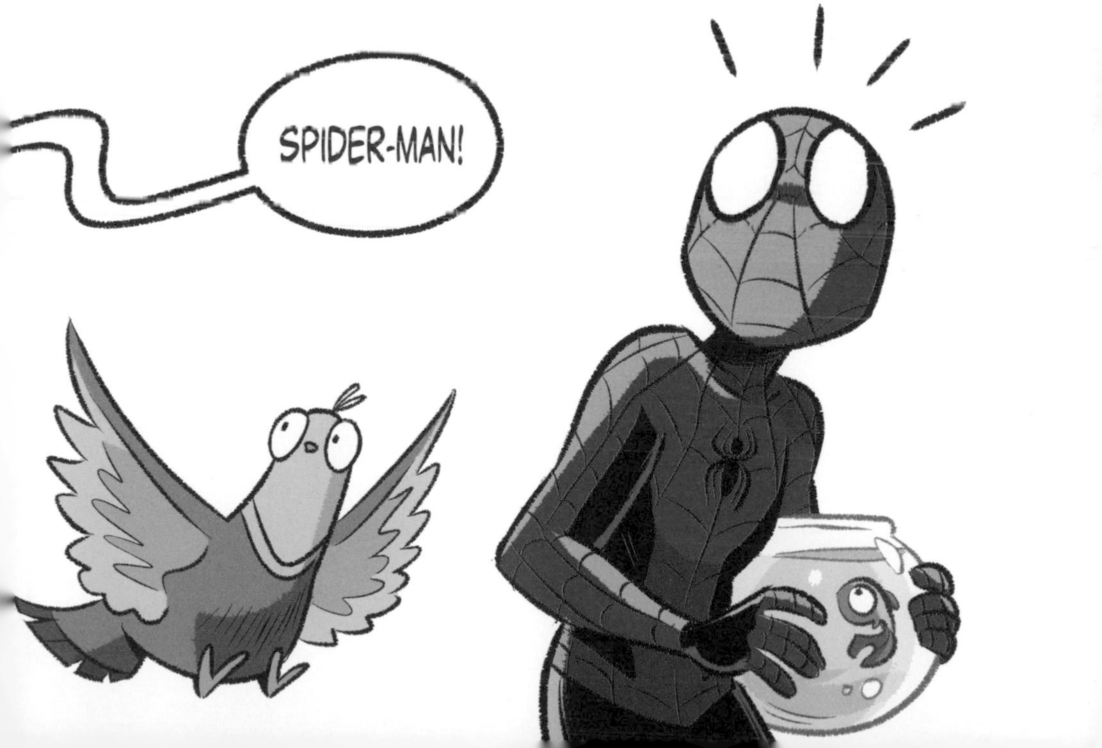
SPIDER-MAN!

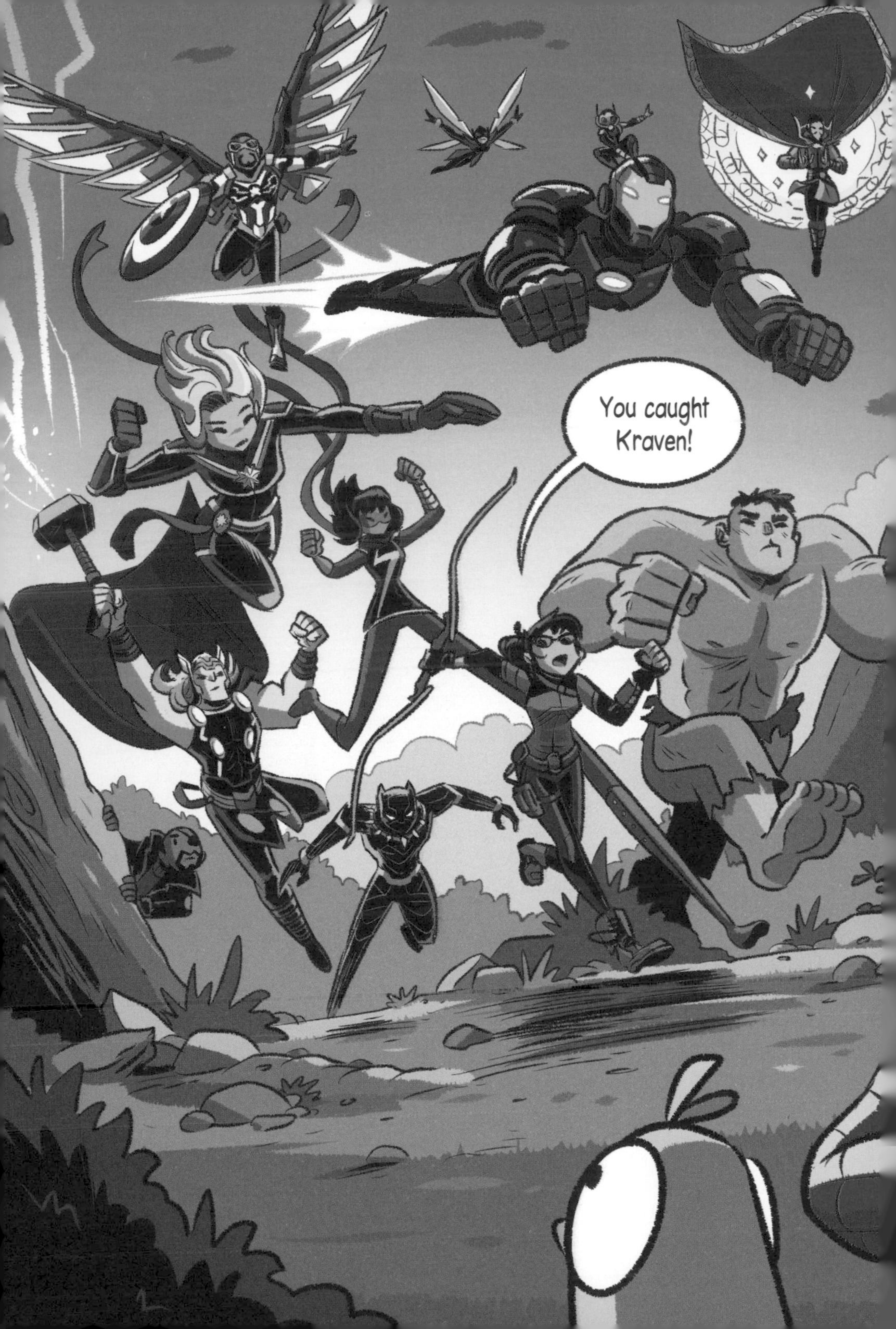
You caught Kraven!

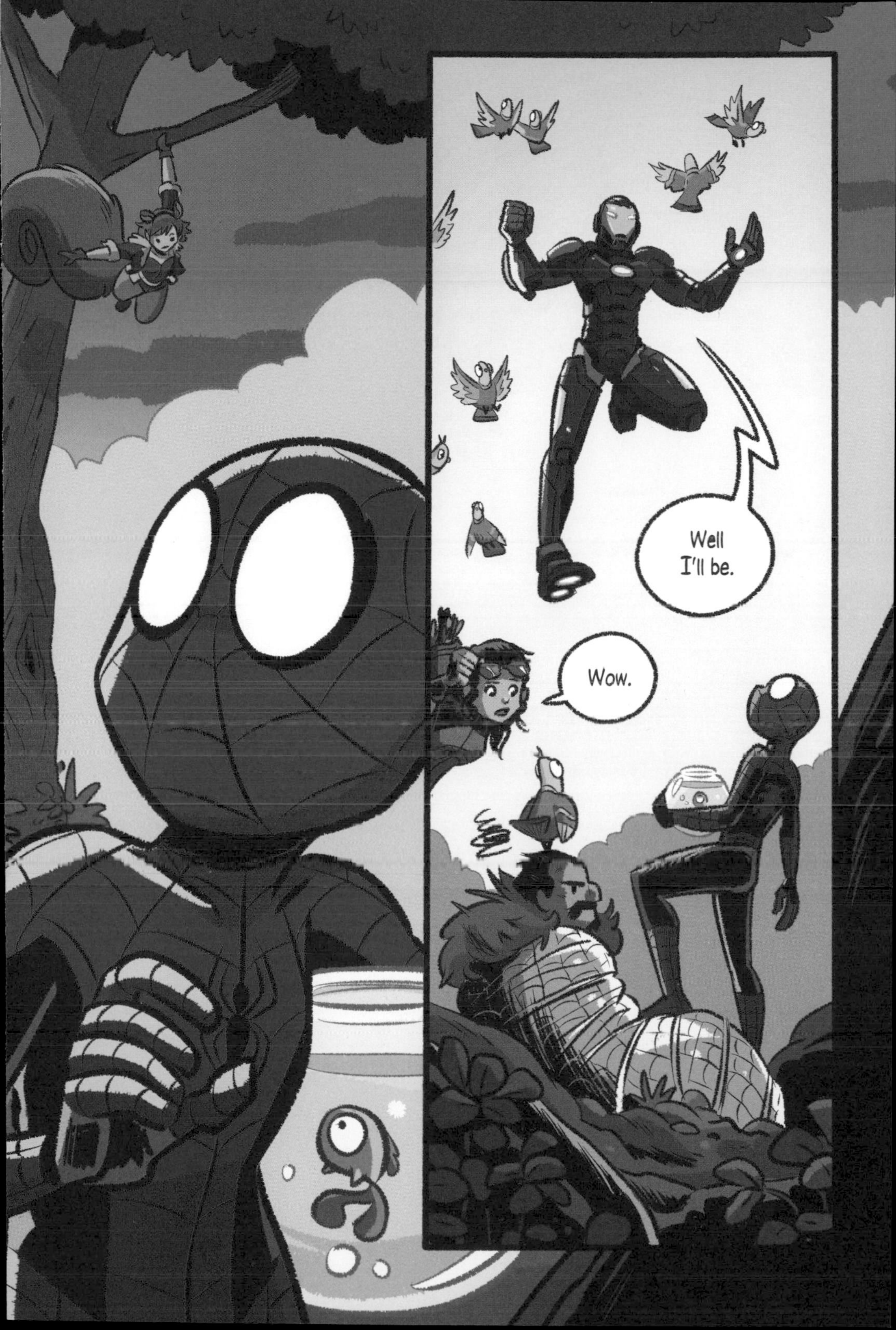
Well I'll be.
Wow.

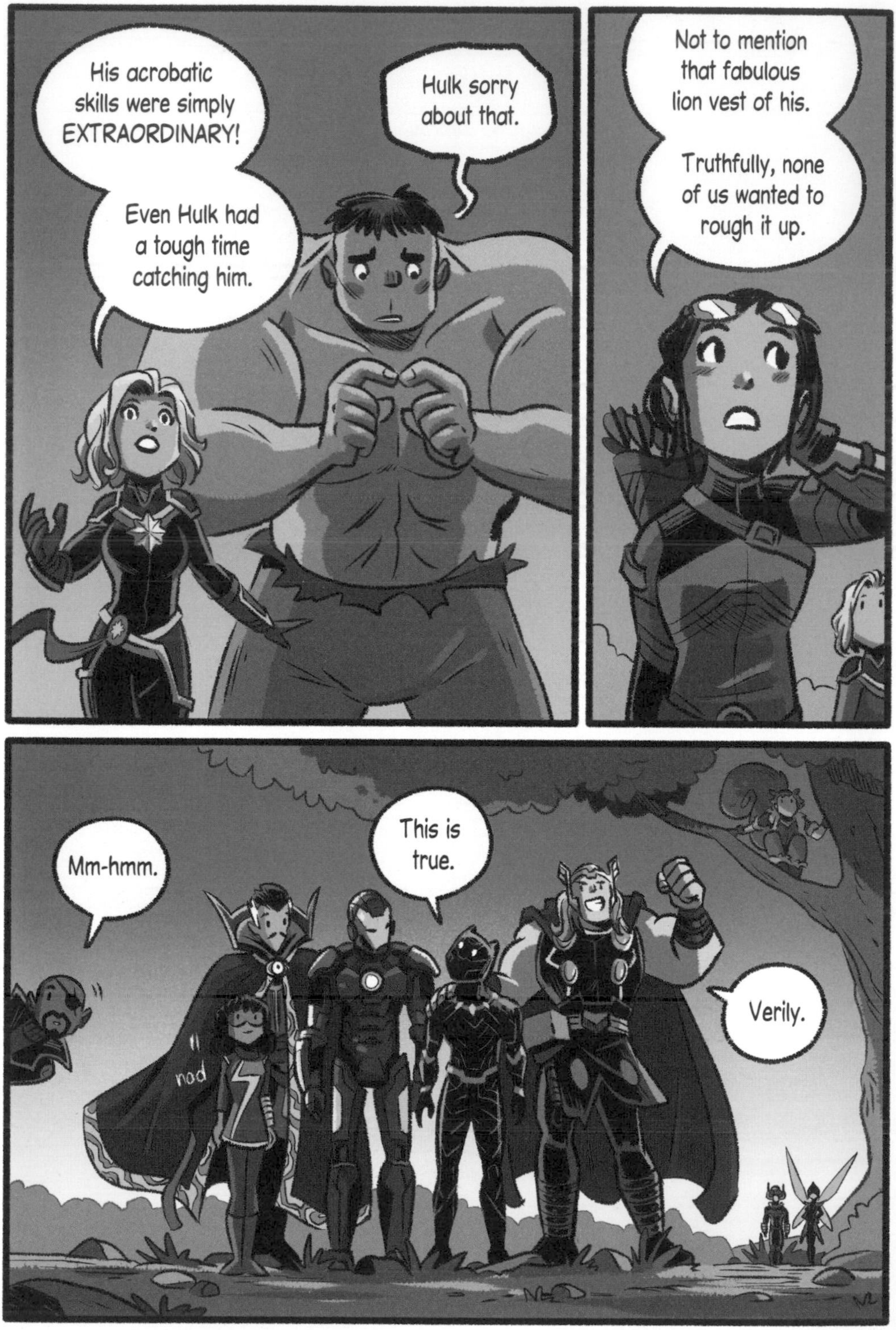

His acrobatic skills were simply EXTRAORDINARY!
Even Hulk had a tough time catching him.
Hulk sorry about that.
Not to mention that fabulous lion vest of his.
Truthfully, none of us wanted to rough it up.
Mm-hmm.
This is true.
Verily.
nod

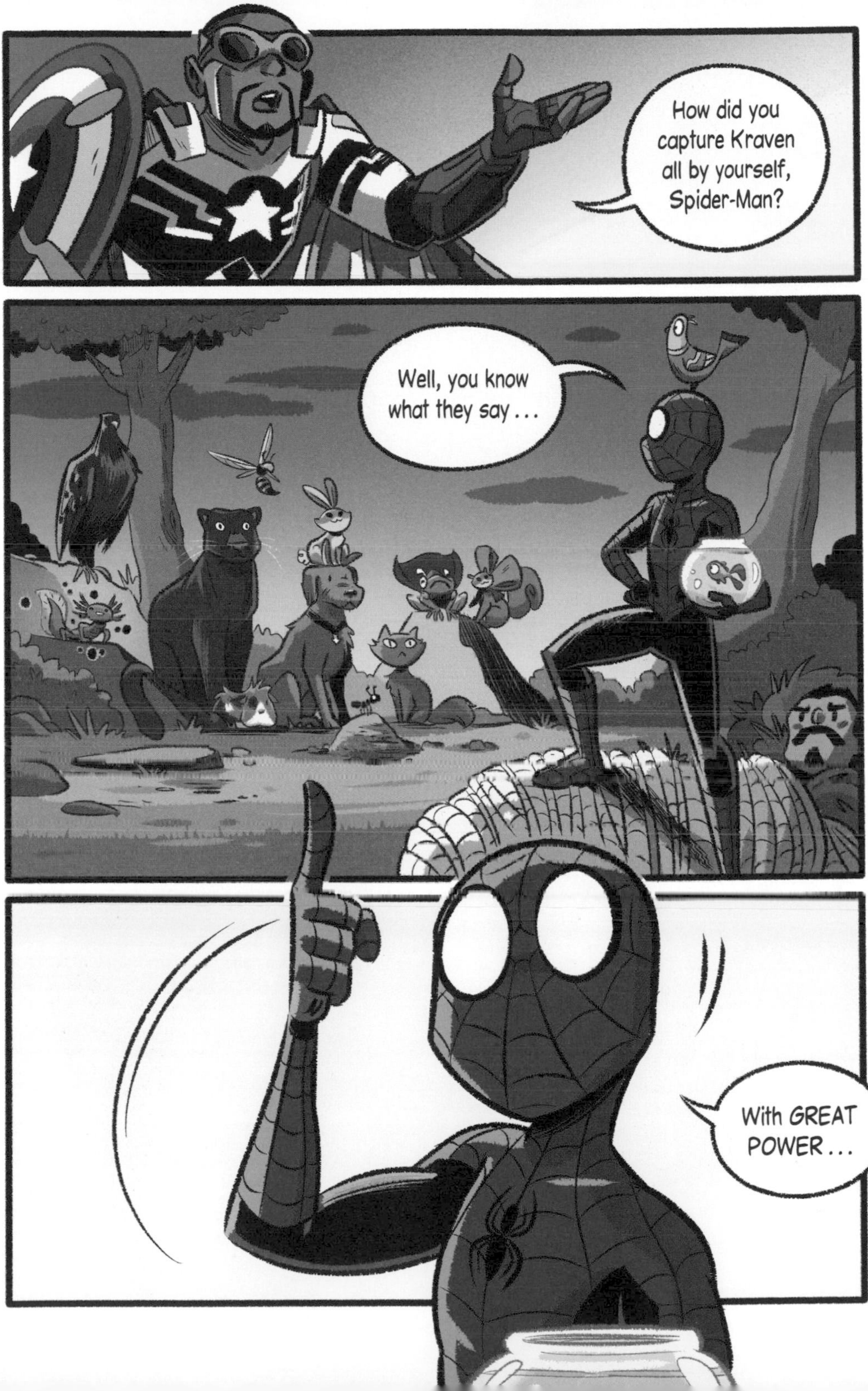
How did you capture Kraven all by yourself, Spider-Man?
Well, you know what they say . . .
With GREAT POWER . . .

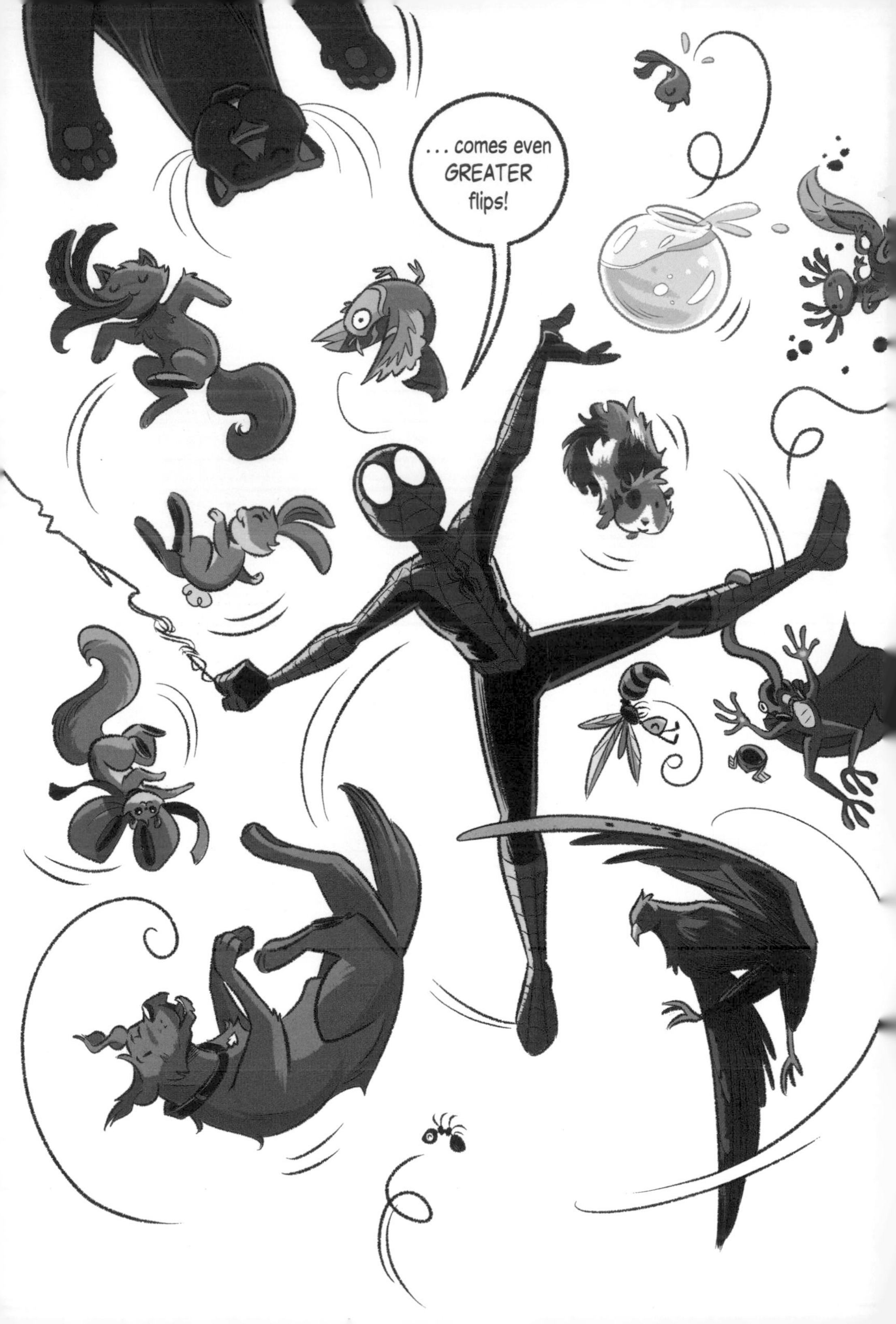
. . . comes even GREATER flips!

# ABOUT THE CREATOR

**Mike Maihack** is a cartoonist best known for his Cleopatra in Space graphic novels published by Scholastic Graphix. The six-book series has earned a Florida Book Award and a starred review from *School Library Journal*, was selected as a YALSA Quick Pick for Reluctant Young Adult Readers, and was produced as a children's animated series by DreamWorks Television.

He has never been able to successfully perform an awesome flip but is actively searching for an ancient talisman that will allow him to do so.

Mike lives in Land O' Lakes, Florida, with his wife, two boys, and two cats. More of his work can be found online at operationspacecat.com.

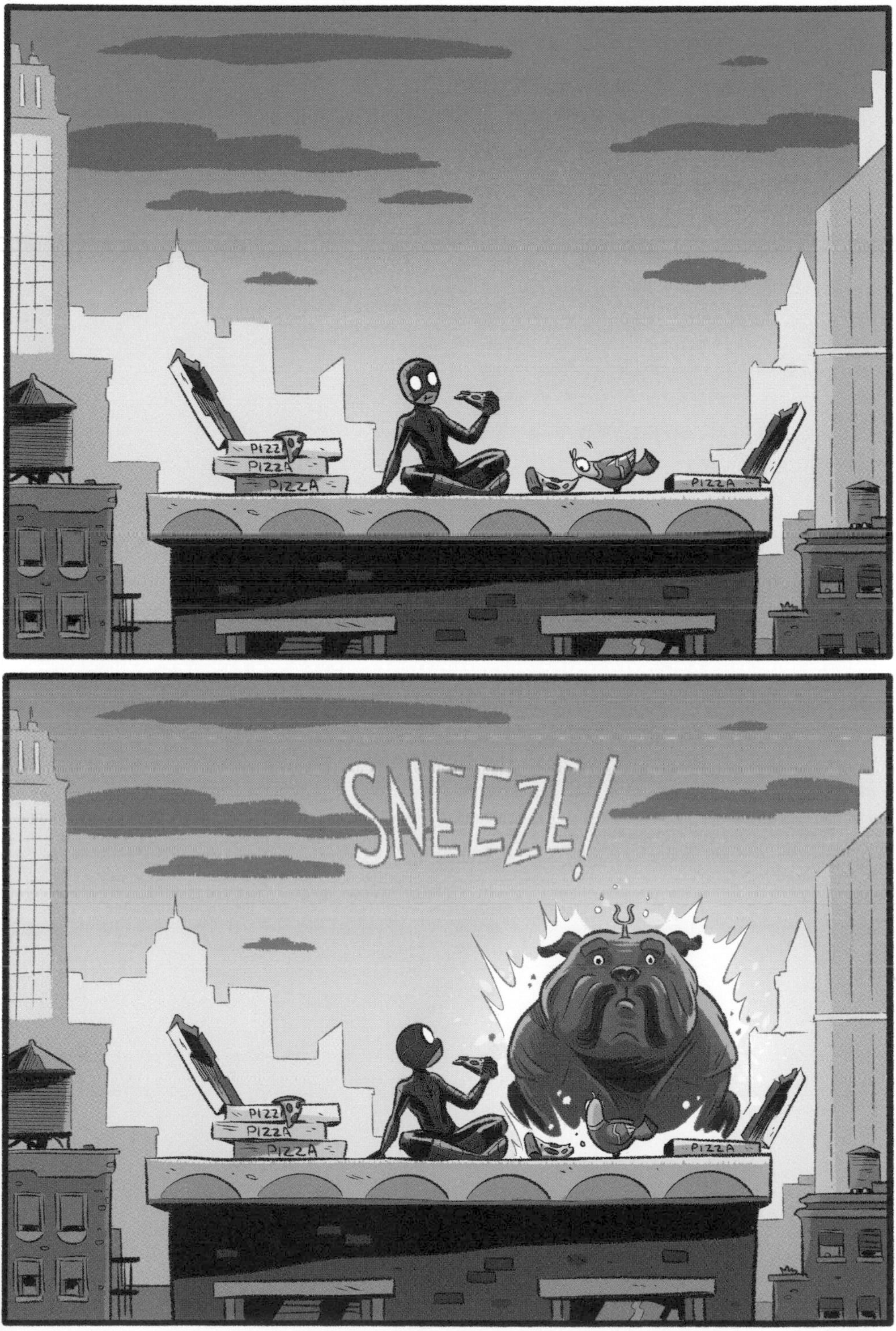
PIZZ
PIZZA
PIZZA
PIZZA
SNEEZE!
PIZZ
PIZZA
PIZZA
PIZZA